LIAM

DOWNIE

PARANORMAL

ORIGINS

THE FORGOTTEN CASE FILES

PARANORMAL ORIGINS

THE FORGOTTEN CASE FILES

PARANORMAL ORIGINS

THE FORGOTTEN CASE FILES

ALSO, BY LIAM K. DOWNIE

PARANORMAL ORIGINS ANTHOLOGY: PHASE ONE

Endurance (Re-release 2020)

Paranormal Origin's: The forgotten Case Files (This Book)

The Rain Man (Coming 2021, under edit)

Isolated (Coming 2021, under edit)

Shadow of Harajuku (Coming 2021)

The Mystery of Hotel Requiem (Coming 2021)

Hypothermia (Coming 2021)

I survived the rapture (2021)

Paranormal Origins: The forgotten case files Phase two (2022)

The *Paranormal Origins* Anthology is a continuous, Ever-expanding collection of horror novels, novellas and shorts that explore every dark corner of the paranormal and the unknown.

Contents

(major stories marked in bold)

DEDICATION

I'd like to dedicate this collection of works to my brother, Mark, and my dad, both of whom have sadly passed away. I'd also like to dedicate to my family who have stood by me through thick and thin, and my friends, even when I myself was at rock bottom and had no faith.

Thank You.

CASE ONE

THE DARK HOUR

ONE

THE WHITE LIGHT of a computer screen illuminates 19-year-old Hope Connors as she sits cross-legged with her auburn hair in a messy bun. She works tirelessly on an essay for her HND graded unit, but with mental fatigue setting in, she pries herself away from the glowing screen. Blinking a few times, to allow her pale blue eyes to adjust to the room around her. It is in many ways the total opposite of herself, messy and bland with few splashes of excitement scattered aimlessly around. There hangs a poster here, a figurine stands over there, and a few small prints of artwork hanging around her bed. The walls are callous and off-white, and her clothes are strewn about carelessly. *Ironic*, she thought, for an art student's room to be so blasé.

However, there is one piece that stands out among the sea of drabness. Something that never fails to catch her attention whenever her focus drifts away from her college work. A picture in a small frame on her nightstand of her when she was much younger. In this photo, she stood smiling astride a man named Henry, but of course, to Hope he was just "Dad".

The photo is a permanent reminder of a beautiful day she and her family had many years before his cancer was diagnosed. He died only two months prior, abruptly and without any real catharsis. Hope was away at school the day he died, the last time they spoke was through a text exchange wherein she sent him a picture she thought he'd think was funny. He simply replied, "ha-ha still coming over tomorrow?" but that very night, he died due to unforeseen complications surrounded only by the panicked screams of Hope's mother, the anxious voices of hospital staff and the shrill alarm tone of machines.

The guilt of her absence burns her soul every time she sees his picture. Even still, she cannot help but lock her eyes on his every time it enters her periphery. She felt tears welling up in her eyes before she heard a loud crash coming from outside her door and down the stairs.

Hope sat up startled and several seconds of tense silence passed, then the furious howl of her mother's voice broke like thunder. "Josh Connors! What the hell did you do?" She shrieked and was met with the wailing cry of her younger brother.

"I'm sorry mum, it was an accident!" Josh stammered out between gasps of air and yowls of crying and fear.

Hope shot out of her bed and rushed through her doorway and down the stairs towards the commotion, with the cacophonous beating of enraged yelling, scared crying, and the nervous barking of their dog growing louder with every step. Her heart raced as she got closer and began being able to distinguish the slew of expletives coming from her mother. She made her way into the kitchen where the uproar was and saw the stage set with both actors standing over broken glass and spilled apple juice. The entire top surface was flooded, Hope looked up and made eye contact with her mother who had momentarily ceased her onslaught to meet Hope's gaze.

Melissa Connors is a tall, gaunt framed woman, 41 years in age. Though truth be told, she looked much older now. In large part due to the traumas of her husband's diagnosis and recent death. Her hair was long and thin, and she never took care of it, so it was constantly tangled and unkempt. Her eyes locked onto Hope's and she could see the venom both she and her brother had become well acquainted with in the last two months. She was once a compassionate woman, and wonderful mother. She was always there in all of Hope's fond memories of her old life standing next to her father, smiling, and laughing. However, now her eyes which once brimmed with life and love now sank hollow into deep bags and emanated a sense of repulsion.

Melissa lashed out in response shoving Josh aside and straight to the floor.

"Clean this mess up this instant, and you," she said making her way over to Hope, "shouldn't you be studying, or some shit?"

"Are you out of your mind? It was accident, don't hit him!" Hope exclaimed trying to push past to her brother's aid, but she was met with the vice grip of her mother's hand around her arm and shoved back into position right in front of her adversary. Hope looked squarely into her unyielding gaze and examined her face. Her facial muscles were twitching with anticipation, and Hope could smell alcohol from her breath.

Melissa had struggled for years with anorexia, but things had become much worse after she lost her husband. Melissa had confided to Hope about it once, long ago. She said she was ashamed but didn't know how to stop herself. She told Hope that if it weren't for her, Henry, and baby Joshua, she wasn't sure if she could bring herself to want to save herself. Unfortunately, when Henry lost his war, Melissa felt she was destined to lose hers as well.

Melissa cut the tension, "Oh? Just an accident? Well, pardon the hell out of me!" Her voice now quivering with anger.

"Mum, stop! Please! This isn't like you!" Hope pleaded, while desperately trying to break free of her mother's grasp.

"Not like me, now is it? What would you know? The only person who ever knew me is dead! Worst of all, the bastard left me with a child too stupid to pour a glass of juice and a know-it-all who's too good for anyone but herself and her damn, useless art degree!"

"Fuck's sake, mum! The loss of dad has been hard for all of us, but we're supposed to be together through this!"

"Don't you dare take that tone with me, you little shit! You think you know so much, but you don't know anything! You've never had to sacrifice anything for anyone! You weren't even there the night he died!"

"You think I don't regret that every day? Every time I see his picture. I would have been there if I had known!"

"Well that doesn't matter now, does it? As far as I'm concerned, your father might have just let himself die so that he didn't have to deal with you two brats!"

Without warning, Melissa finally snapped. Months of pent up aggression and resentment had reached their zenith. In one swift motion, Melissa reeled her arm back and swung forward, striking Hope across her face with such force that it nearly knocked her off balance. Burning embarrassment and shock ran through Hope as tears began welling up in her eyes. Tears of frustration and anger. She kept her attention focused on the ground; she could not bear to look at her mother, considering this was the first and only time Melissa had every physically punished her or Josh.

From the other room, the continuous barking of the family's German shepherd, Tara, exploded into a frenzy as she sprinted into the kitchen and made her stance between Melissa and Hope. Melissa knew now with certainty, everyone in the house was against her. With her anger still seething, she reeled back once again and kicked Tara hard enough that the dog's shrill yelp might have been heard all the way back into town. Tara was not an aggressive dog, and even after being assaulted, she did not retaliate, instead she merely got back up and moved back over to Hope's side.

Hope had recovered from her daze and she made her way over to Josh. He stood motionless throughout the whole ordeal, obviously traumatized by everything he had just experienced. In one evening, his whole world had been shattered.

"Come on, Josh. Mum isn't feeling well right now, so we're going outside until she cools off, okay?" Hope said, kneeling to look him in the face.

His skin was pale, and his once vibrant eyes were now devoid of life. Slowly, he turned his head to Hope and wordlessly nodded. Melissa at this point, merely huffed and sat herself down in the chair at the opposite end of the dining room and held her head in her hands.

Hope told Josh to go to his room and change into hiking clothes and meet her at the front door. Hope herself changed into black jeans, well-worn boots, a pair of warm fingerless gloves, and the light brown coat her father bought her.

She looked into her mirror and instantly saw that she also wore her mother's pale red handprint on her cheek. She put her hand up to it and recoiled when she felt its burning and soreness.

As she stepped outside her room, she found Josh waiting for her wearing his favorite navy-blue jacket, a hat, and a pair of his own gloves. Hope could feel his confused stare on her bruise. She put on a smile and rustled her fingers through his messy brown hair and motioned for him to follow her downstairs. Tara was waiting patiently at the foot of the staircase and shot up with her tail wagging when she saw them.

Hope used a silly voice to ask if perhaps Tara would like to accompany them, and her eyes lit up as she ran to the door to impatiently wait for them. Usually, Tara's excitement is contagious and puts a smile on Josh's face, so Hope looked back at him expectantly but saw his eyes solemnly fixed to the ground in front of him as he walked towards the door. Hope handed Josh the leash that she attached to Tara and led them out the door first.

She took one final look into the kitchen as the pair passed her and saw her mother sitting there with a bottle of liquor in front of her, mumbling incoherently. Hope made a deep sigh, and followed Josh and Tara, locking the door behind her. Her thoughts raced about what was to come next; what happens when they come back? Should they even **COME BACK AT ALL?**

TWO

THE FAIRY TRAIL

THE NEW life the Connors thought that their new home would offer them was not the one any of them had dreamed it would be. The former mining village of Rivenside was quaint, scenic, and mostly devoid of the distractions that city living came with. The idea for moving here after Henry's death was so that the family would be closer together. Hope could do most of her college work online, Josh would start at his new school in the fall, and Melissa would be able to stop seeing signs of Henry and the life they used to lead. That was the idea, but the truth simply was that there was no distance too great for grief to follow, nor any panorama too beautiful to hold together a failing family.

That said, Rivenside was gorgeous, for a former mining town. Rumors floated around the town square the people didn't come to Rivenside anymore after some great plague swept across the inhabitants and killed more than half the town over the course of only a few weeks; but of course, they were only rumors. There was no concrete evidence anywhere of any mysterious plague, though curiously, the once thriving village was in truth seemingly vacated overnight and most of its history vanished alongside the villagers. However, that was all that Hope cared to have read about this place when she first arrived. She paid little mind to the villagers or its history, for she was certain that once she was finished with her degree, she would take a nice job in the city and move back to where life was more vibrant.

Though, even for all its dullness, Hope was admittedly infatuated with the natural beauty of its landscape. Thus, she spent many evenings wandering the surrounding woodland around her home. On her many ventures, she found something as strange as it was enchanting, a fairy trail that she was certain would put Josh at ease. With Tara at the lead, they had reached their destination. On a rickety, overgrown portcullis a dingy sign read "Rivenside Fairy Trail".

Hope looked down at Josh and saw him peeking through the passageway at the winding dirt trails and tall brush all littered with old toys. Hope begins to walk forward with Josh's hand in hers before she feels a gentle tug back and feels his fingers tighten softly around her palm. She turns around and notices him standing perfectly still looking up at her until he finally opens his mouth.

"Hope? Is it my fault that Mum's angry all the time? Am I the reason Dad died?" he asked with a lump in his throat as his eyes began to water.

"Oh, Josh, no!" Hope responded without delay as she knelt to meet his gaze; she felt the radiating heat from her facial bruise flare up as tears of her own began to bead up in the corners of her eyes. "It is not your fault, okay? Don't ever blame yourself for something like that. Mum isn't feeling very well, and it sometimes makes her say and do things that she doesn't mean."

Josh nodded subtly in agreement, "So things will be okay when we go home?"

"I promise. Now come on, let's go exploring."

For the first time that evening the two shared a warm embrace and felt a genuine sense of comfort as a pair of warm smiles crept over their faces. After a few moments, Hope raised herself up and playfully squeezed Josh's hand and motioned for them to begin their adventure. They ran excitedly through the gate and down one of the dirt trails with Tara following close behind them.

They played with toys, made jokes, and spoke in funny voices until they were red in the face from laughter. They made their way deep into the woods until the childlike wonder of the fairy trail began to become scarce. All of a sudden, there was a snap of a branch somewhere to the side of them off the main trail. Tara began to growl ferociously with her fur raised all the way up. Hope pulled Josh in close while looking out into the darkness, occasionally glancing down to Tara seeing her bare her fangs at an invisible stalker. Hope calls to Tara in an attempt to calm her down and begins to walk with Josh down a splintering path away from where Tara was barking. Tara eventually calmed her barking and followed them but would turn her head every now and again to growl or let out a low bark.

The path they were now following was pitch black, though Hope did her best to keep Josh calm, she too was becoming increasingly nervous about whatever it was that startled Tara. She found herself constantly looking over her shoulder expecting to see someone following them through the trees, but there was nothing except vegetation dimly illuminated in the moonlight. Eventually the dense overhang of trees gave way to a perfectly circular clearing whose only focal point was a massive broken-down tree painted in the pale moonlight. The tree must have collapsed some time ago, Hope speculated, since the branches had no leaves and its bark was petrified.

Curiously, Hope noticed that at its base was a hollow spot that looked unnatural, as if someone had hollowed it out by hand. As she approached, she noticed that it was large enough for her and Josh to both comfortably stand inside. She motioned for Josh to follow her inside and **HE RELUCTANTLY FOLLOWED.**

THREE

THE SHRINE

UPON ENTERING the tree, Hope and Josh examined the interior of the hollow and saw that it had been carefully and masterfully maintained. Its walls were perfectly smooth, and to look around, Hope felt like she was standing in a temple, rather than a hollow tree. She inspected the walls carefully and saw that dozens of symbols had been carved into it from ceiling to floor. Try as she might though, she could not make heads or tails of what they were supposed to be.

They looked vaguely like some kind of foreign language, but nothing Hope had ever seen before. There was a sort of order to them that she felt made them cohesive, but the longer she tried to decipher them, the more otherworldly they became to her. Hope snapped back to reality when she heard Josh make a small, audible gasp.

"What's up? Find something?" Hope asked as she walked closer to Josh.

"I thought this was another toy, but its kind of creepy looking." Josh said as he turned around and extended his open hands to Hope.

He held a small figurine. Hope gingerly picked it up and looked intensely at it. It was expertly carved into wood, presumably the same as the tree, and it was vaguely humanlike. It had two arms and two legs, but they were inhumanly long reaching down and curling over its squared base. It had four long appendages that reached up from out of its shoulders and curled up over its head.

Its top half and lower half were connected only by a thin line of wood that resembled a spinal column. Its head was featureless but smooth, except for two small indentations that had been painted black where its eyes would be. Hope noticed that the paint was relatively fresh, as it was still running down the icon's face as she moved it around.

"Hope look, there's something else here that was under it." Josh exclaimed as he held up a thin piece of cloth for Hope to look at, "It says something, but I don't know what some of the words mean. Can you read it for me?" he continued with a tinge of nervousness in his voice.

"Of course, may I see it?" Hope asked extending her hand, Josh complied and handed it over for her to read.

"The salt of tears beckons the Dark Hour

First comes the ringing of invisible bells

Closed eyes will glimpse the world unseen

A storm of wind and rain will find you

Then the beast will call for you

Open your eyes and make your escape

Make haste lest the hunter catch its prey

Should the rabbit escape the wolf

It will find all it has lost"

Hope looked curiously at the document for a while then back to Josh.

"What does that last line mean?" Josh asked anxiously.

"I think it means that if you do what it says you can get something back that you lost." Hope said with a hint of skepticism and confusion.

"Do you think we could get Dad back?" There was moment's silence before hope gave a response.

"Josh... I wish life worked like that. I know it's unfair, but we must accept that dad isn't coming back. He wouldn't want us stuck in the past, he'd want us to look forward to the future and live a happy life in his memory. Do you understand?"

"But the paper said we could if we just-"

"Josh, no. I don't want you thinking there's some magic spell that's going to bring him back."

"You're not even listening!"

"Josh, I said that's enough. Now come on."

Hope put the figure in his hands and turned to briskly walk away. She hated shutting him down so decisively, but she felt that letting him go on thinking that their lives would ever go back to the way they were, magic or no magic, would do more harm than good.

She stepped out of the wood hollow and made only a few steps before she realized Josh had not followed her out. Tara, who had been waiting patiently outside, stood up and tilted her head also noticing that Hope was alone. Hope then whipped her head back around and saw that Josh had turned around to face back into the center of the tree.

"Josh!" Hope called out but was met with no response.
She stepped through the entrance of the shrine and called out to him again. This time he turned around toward the sound of her voice but continued to stand motionless. She opened her mouth to call once again then she heard something strange, like a bell from far away. Its tone was quiet, but high pitched, and sustained a constant hum.

Hope whipped her head around but saw nothing through the trees except for Tara who now stood with her fur raised up; she began growling once again. Hope turned her head back to Josh and raised her phone's light towards him. She illuminated him and saw that his eyes were closed, and he was holding the figurine tightly in his hands. He had tears streaming quickly down his face, as they cascaded down his chin they fell squarely onto the effigy.

"Josh! Put that thing down and come over here!" Hope screamed, now equal parts unnerved and frustrated.

"No!" He yelled at the top of his lungs, pinching his eyes closed even tighter.

"Josh! I swear to god, I'm not asking you again!"

"I just want things to go back to normal!"
Just as the words left his mouth, a booming crack of thunder echoed out from behind them. It was quickly followed by a sudden, inexplicable downpour. The fallen tree offered little shelter as Hope and Josh were quickly soaked in the torrent.

Hope heard Tara start barking madly, but as she turned to look at her, she only saw her sprinting away into the woods. Hope decided she had enough, and she lunged towards Josh and grabbed the wooden idol from his hands. As her fingers wrapped around it, she heard a new sound which shook her to her core.

She heard an otherworldly screeching sound surrounded by disembodied, pained whisperings. Their voices were indistinguishable from one another in an unhallowed cacophony, but she could manage to make out at least one of the voices.

The voice was that of her mother, and as she focused in on it, her vision blurred until she saw a vignette of the scene that had transpired that very evening.

She heard her biting words once again, watching the spectacle unfold from the outside, like watching a film. She saw her mother lean back, and swing at her, and her face began to burn a searing pain. The vision faded away as quickly as it appeared, then from the moaning wail of voices she heard another which she had not heard in some time.

It was the voice of her father, then just as before with her mother, she saw her father. He was sickly with tubes and wires coming out of him in every direction, she realized quickly she was in the hospital room with him. His haggard face had a look of anguish as he weakly struggled in his bed. Then the high-pitched whine of his heart monitor pierced her ears. She saw her mother standing over him, with panic in her eyes as nurses and doctors poured into the room, but she knew it was too late.

The scene quickly snapped to his funeral and she saw herself sitting between her mother and Josh. She saw the nervous confusion on Josh's face, then she looked over to herself and saw how red her eyes were from crying. She then looked over to her mother, and though she wouldn't have noticed at the time, she saw that her mother's eyes were not facing forward, rather they were aimed pointedly sideways, burning with a vague sense of anger. She realized it was at that very moment that her mother started to foster her resentment towards her and her brother. The scene faded out once again, and all at once, the clamor of voices and the unyielding screeching suddenly came to a halt.

Her vision turned to a brilliant, pulsing red, which began to swirl around her, like blood flowing down a drain. The color began to fade until she was left with utter blackness. Then, she noticed a metallic taste on her lips and a pungent odor in the air. Her eyes opened slowly, and as her senses all came back, she was met with a feeling of overwhelming dread and a sense of dire **URGENCY**.

FOUR

THE OTHER WORLD

HOPE FINDS HERSELF face down on the floor of the tree's cavern. Her head is pounding and her bones ache, but she lifts herself up and examines her surroundings. She notices instantly that she is alone. Both Josh and Tara are nowhere to be seen, and all she can hear is the gentle patter of rain on the tree's exterior and the whisper of wind as it breaks against its surface. Steadying herself against the wall, she sluggishly makes her way out and into the clearing. The world that meets her is painted with a dull, rusty hue as she looks to the sky and sees a blood red sky with a black moon at its zenith.

As the rain continues to fall on her face, she realizes that what is falling isn't water, but blood. Her mind races trying to make sense of what is happening. She pulls up her phone hoping to see an online news article about some strange meteorological occurrence that might explain her current situation but finds that she has no signal. She attempts to call her house to see if perhaps Josh and Tara had returned home, but she is met only with a strange static tone she's never heard before. She hangs up quickly and turns her light on. With a sigh of exasperation, she anxiously makes her way back the way she came through the woods.

Much of the world around is her is as she remembers but as she scans her surroundings, she sees the same strange symbols that lined the walls of the tree hollow carved into stones and crudely fashioned out of sticks dangling from branches. As she continues down the trail, suddenly she hears a sticky, damp sound as she steps firmly onto some kind of puddle. Hope stops in her track and shines her light downward at her foot. She lifts her shoe up with some resistance and sees a trail of viscous, red ichor from her foot to the ground. Despite the fact that the world was literally raining blood, none of it had congealed so solidly into a singular, large puddle on the flat ground.

She shined her light forward and saw that it left a noticeable trail, as if something had been dragged through it. She cautiously followed the trail until a foreign object entered her light. She wasn't sure what it was, but it was fleshy and covered in blood. With her hands now violently trembling she continued following the blood further up the dirt path until it stopped at the base of a tall tree. She saw another smaller puddle of blood forming at its base then saw a

25

large droplet of blood fall into it. Then another one. She quickly shined her phone up into its branches and saw its origin.

Hope let out a shrill gasp, followed by a whimpering utterance of guttural sound as she examined the mangled corpse of her dog Tara. She had been impaled on a sharp branch with her chest cut open from her throat down to her stomach. Her innards were strewn about carelessly around the adjoining branches, but it looked as though whatever did this, took her heart with it, as that was the only organ missing from the grizzly scene.

Hope fell to her knees and covered her mouth with her hand, feeling the rush of bile as she struggled to not be sick. She tried to be silent fearing that whatever did this may still be lurking nearby, but she could not silence herself completely as she broke down and began crying profusely. Not long after, she hears a familiar sound.

"Hope! Are you there? Help me, I'm scared!" the voice of Josh rang out from far away, further into the denseness of the woods.

She lifted her face up with elation, but her hopes were quickly dashed as Josh's voice were answered by another familiar sound. A bloodcurdling screech loosed from behind the tree line behind her. She recognized the inhuman shriek from when she touched the idol; it was like nothing she'd ever heard before from animal, man, nor machine. Her blood froze in her veins, but she knew she had to hide lest she suffer the same fate as Tara. She made a mad dash into some nearby low-lying brush and laid down with her flashlight off and her hands over her mouth to silence her panicked breathing.

The creature emerged from the shadows without a sound. It stood hunched forward but still at a towering ten feet high. It looked humanoid, but its arms and legs were easily twice as long as a normal human's, with jagged nails reaching several inches away from each finger's apex. Its chest was nearly just exposed rib cage and spinal column, but upon inspection was covered with thin, leathery skin pulled tightly across. An eerie black glow emanated from its back where several ghostly tendrils gently swayed back and forth, unphased by gravity. Its head was nearly featureless except for a pair of empty eye sockets where thick, black ooze continually poured out, cascading down its face and body. Its mouth had no lips, exposing its bloodstained, crooked teeth.

The sight of the creature sent Hope's senses into retreat as she tried to comprehend what she was witnessing. She recalled the form of the idol in the tree and realized it was an effigy of the monstrosity before her. Its filthy maw opened up suddenly as it unleashed another horrifying screech, splitting her ear drums, causing her to close her eyes and begin holding her breath.

She kept her eyes closed as she heard it begin to make movements near the tree where Tara was. She heard it clambering up the trunk with little effort, then she heard the nauseating sound as it began to consume the remains. Every gnash of its teeth and every ripping sound of flesh from bone made Hope sick to her stomach. She feverishly resisted the urge to vomit, fearing that it would turn its attention to her. Just as began to wonder what would happen next, Josh cried out yet again, this time slightly closer.

"Hope! Please! Help me!" He cried out; Hope could tell he was crying by the wavering of his voice and the desperation of his tone.

She so desperately wanted to call out to warn him to run and hide. She wanted to jump out and run to his aid so that she might protect him, but fear kept her still. In her head she berated herself for not having the bravery to go out and save her brother, but she knew deep down if she made a break for him now, it would mean certain death for them both. She had to wait until the creature was gone so she could make her move.

As Josh continued to frantically cry out, the creature's attention shifted away from its meal. It let out another chilling screech and leapt away from the tree branches into the darkness towards his direction. Now truly feeling the urgency, Hope cast away her hesitation and sprinted after the creature toward Josh. She knew his life was in her hands, and as far as she was concerned, there was no force above or below that would keep her from **PROTECTING HIM**.

FIVE

THE HUNTER AND THE PREY

HOPE RUSHED feverishly through the woods, looking for any sign of her brother. Along the way, she'd see snapped branches and claw marks on stone and bark. She had never been more afraid of anything in her life, not more than her father dying nor returning home to her abusive life with their mother. Even still, she did not slow her advance. She wasn't afraid of being maimed and eviscerated, she was afraid of losing the only person she had left in this world, the only one she genuinely cared about. Josh.

Eventually she came across a strange structure she had never seen in her many trips through these woods. She wiped the bloody rain from her eyes and inspected the building. She knew Josh would be clever enough to hide if he knew the creature was pursuing him, so she hurried up to the entrance and looked in. She heard a quiet sobbing and cautiously approached its origin. She found Josh huddled under a small wooden table with his head tucked into his knees, rocking back and forth on his feet.

She reached over and touched him on the shoulder and as his head shot up in fright, she muffled his surprised yelp with her other hand. His eyes darted all over her and after he was certain it was really her; he threw his arms around her waist in a tight hug. After a moment's reprieve, she peeled him away holding a finger to her lips to signify that they needed to be quiet. No sooner than that, they hear the creature unleash its screech from outside the building, followed by a massive thud on the roof of the structure.

They heard huffing and moaning as it crawled all around. They hid tightly in the shadows, careful to not make any noise. After a while, the creature was convinced its prey was not to be found and let out a low, pained growl as it made one last powerful leap away into the trees.

Josh released Hope then quickly rifled through his pockets revealing a small piece of parchment. He handed it over to Hope and began to speak.

"It's just like the one we saw before. I tried reading it, but I don't get it."

"Okay, let me read it; maybe it tells us how we can get out of here."

Hope began reading each line carefully hoping it would be clearer cut than the one before it. To her relief, this was more a set of instructions rather than an esoteric poem.

"It says,

'Dear, oh dear, you've found your way here?

You want to go home before being ripped flesh from bone?

Go back to the tree to escape the powers that be

Shed salty tears to make the nightmare disappear'

"So, all we have to do is go back to that tree shrine and cry some tears onto this paper, then close our eyes, right?"

Josh nodded his head quickly, now revitalized with hope and vigor.

"Okay then, Josh, stay very close to me and do exactly as I tell you and we'll go home together. Got it?"

He answered her by giving her another solid hug, which she reciprocated whole heartedly. It did not take them long to get back to the dirt trail leading down to the tree. They exercised the utmost caution and stayed hidden in the shadows but saw no sign of the creature; even stranger still, they did not hear its call. But as they approached the moon lit clearing, now caked in blood, it became abundantly clear as to why.

The creature was waiting for them. It sat perched atop the tree, scouring the tree line in search of its prey. Josh was visibly terrified, but Hope kept her gaze fixed to the creature, carefully watching its every movement. Its ethereal tendrils wrapped and unwrapped from around each other, the black drip from its eyes fell to the ground, and it methodically raked its claws against the wood. Hope looked closely and saw that the creature itself was carving the symbols they had seen in the tree and throughout the surrounding area.

Hope began to wonder that if the creature was intelligent, did it have some part in writing the ritual that brought them here? And if it did, were they falling directly into its trap? There was no time to hypothesize, as the creature began looking around more fervently, Hope was sure that meant it knew they were close and was simply trying to figure out where they were. It was no longer a matter of 'if' it would catch them, it was now a matter of 'when'. Hope pulled Josh in close and began to speak to him.

"Josh, I have a plan, but I know you won't like it." She began, watching his eyes widen with anxiety. "We won't be able to sneak by it with it sitting up there waiting for us. Take the paper you found and wait for me to make a distraction. I'm going to get it to chase me away then you go in and do what it says to do."

"No! You said we'd stay together, don't leave me!"

"I won't. I'll hide once I get far enough away, then once I give it the slip I'll come back and do the ritual too and I'll meet you on the other side, okay?"

Josh looked away from her to get eyes on the creature but once centered in his view his face grew pale and he could not help but look away. Hope began to stand up into a low crouch and move away from him, but she felt his hand wrap around her coat and give a gentle tug.

"You promise you're coming back?" He said with tears beginning to well up in his eyes.

A moment passes and she replies feeling a single tear race down her cheek, "Promise."

She quickly makes her way far enough that she can no longer see Josh through the brush. She stops for a minute, entertaining a fleeting thought of simply running away but she knows that was not an option.

She turned to put the monster in her sight then she let out a yell. She yelled as loud as she could and began to make a dash away from the clearing. Her gambit worked, and the beast responded with its own yell then dropped to the ground to take off after her.

She ran as fast and hard as she could, but she felt the creature quickly gaining on her. She turned her head to take one final look at Josh as she saw him make his way to the tree hollow. She knew in her heart she would not survive, but knowing that Josh would, redoubled her resolve, and gave her a **SENSE OF INNER PEACE.**

SIX

THE DARK HOUR

HOPE KEPT running until her lungs burned and her legs felt like they might give out. She knew the creature was right on top of her but could not bear to look back. She focused in on her hearing but no longer heard footsteps behind her. Had it given up the chase? Or did it turn around at some point to pursue Josh instead? The latter thought mortified her, so she slowed her escape with the intention of turning back around. But no sooner did she stop that a wild rustling came through the wood and without warning the creature erupted from the darkness and struck at her with its tendrils. The impact stripped her of her breath and sent her careening through the air a significant distance away.

The pain was more intense than anything she had ever experienced, leaving a throbbing, burning pain all throughout her body; it reminded her of her mother. In an act of desperation, she crawled away from the creature toward a pointed branch that had been broken off. Perhaps savoring the hunt, the creature walked slowly over to her, maybe even taking joy in her suffering and fear. Just as Hope reached for the branch, the creature quickened its pace and lunged for her exposing its elongated teeth; though fortune favored her, she got a hand around it and had just enough time to turn around on her back and brace herself with the jagged edge toward the creature.

The point pierced through its leathery hide, spraying a torrent of black liquid from its wound over her. It cries out and stops briefly but was otherwise unphased. It quickly wrapped its hand around the spear and tossed it aside, and with no more defenses, picked up Hope by the throat. She felt its long fingers tightening with supernatural strength as its nails dug into her skin, ripping it with ease.

The burn was indescribably painful, but with airway totally constricted, all she could do was writhe in agony as the creature locked its inky black eyes onto hers. Finally, it lashed her body away with her limbs twisting around and bones breaking from the force of impact against dirt and stones. Her body was numb, she knew the pain was immeasurable, but she felt nothing now. Her vision faded in and out and through the ringing she heard in her ears, she heard the creature unleash one more terrible screech as it went in for the kill.

It ran at her motionless body and wrapped its monstrous hands around her head and began to mash it into a nearby tree, repeatedly. She felt the pressure and she saw the blood spattering outwards; she knew it must have been painful. The creature exposed its teeth once again and she saw as they grew pointed and long, then she watched helplessly as it jabbed its face forward into her neck, taking a massive bite out of her shoulder and at the same time it sank its razor sharp claws into her chest and ripped her chest cavity wide open. She was clinging onto the last thread of her life, thinking about her father, her mother, Tara – Josh and her friends as her life flashed before her. Amidst it all, she heard a sound that filled her with dread, it was hard to make out who or what it was, but she was sure it was Josh's voice. His voice echoing from the darkness.

"Hope! I can't do it! I can't…I don't know what to do!" He exclaimed, but she could not physically respond. The creature lifted its head away from her, and as her vision faded to black, she saw it dash away just as fast as it descended upon her. She heard the creature let out one last whale, then there was silence. Hope Connors died holding on to one final thought.

"I'M SORRY, JOSH…"

THE END

CAJE TWO

A PLATFORM SHROUDED IN FOG

MARKUS HOLLOWAY sat down with a huff in the chair outside of his manager's office. He looked up at the clock and through weary eyes made out the time to be 9:47pm. His shift was slated to end at 10pm, but his manager, Tom, told him to see him before he left. He knew he was a bit early but hoped that since it was only his first day that Tom might cut him some slack and let him leave a few minutes early. Markus had never worked as a security guard before, but the position at the Requiem Hotel seemed cushy and paid well enough that he felt mostly comfortable.

He was a well-built man and having been in his fair share of scraps in his younger days, he knew he could hold his own. However, for the crowd at the Requiem, he knew his tough exterior, including a noticeable scar over his right eyebrow, would be more than enough to deter any kind of escalated confrontation.

Finally, the door to the office opened and Tom peaked out to wave him inside. Tom was an older man in his fifties, and despite having some weight in his gut and gray in his hair, he had air of confidence and quiet strength about him that reminded Markus of his own father. He walked around to his seat and Markus sat in the chair facing him. Tom began shuffling some papers he had cluttered all around his desk and finally spoke.

"So, Markus, how'd you find your first shift?" Tom said in a monotone and tired voice.

"I enjoyed it; it was definitely something new. Much better than the place I was working before." Markus replied in a similar tone.

"Glad to hear it; I know it isn't the most exciting place, but you get back what you give, so if you treat this place well, it'll do the same for you."

"So, when am I in next?"
Tom handed him a sheet of paper he pulled from the stack he had just finished organizing,

"Tomorrow, Wednesday, Thursday, and Friday. You'll be backshift, so make sure you plan accordingly."

"Yes, that won't be a problem. Was there anything else you wanted to discuss with me, or am I free to leave?"

"No, you're good to go; I just wanted to touch base and see how you were feeling after your first day. Take care, and I'll see you tomorrow evening."

Markus extended his hand to give Tom a quick handshake before he made his way out of the office. He went downstairs behind the reception desk to pick up his brown leather jacket and his bag carrying his laptop, lunchbox, and other small personal effects.

He began making his way outside the building, giving cordial head nods and "see-you-tomorrows to his colleagues as he passed them by. As he made his way outside, he stopped at the front door to give himself a quick once over in the reflection of the glass. His brown eyes were puffy from the long night, his tanned skin looked slightly pale, and he quickly combed his short black hair back into place and ran his fingers over his chin to feel the prickles of his stubble. He felt about as rundown as he looked so he pushed out of the double doors at the entrance of the hotel and began his pilgrimage home where he might get some much-needed rest.

The night air greeted him with a slight breeze and nip of chilliness. It danced around his face as he walked, stinging his nose and throat with every breath he took. He tightened himself up, then quickened his pace as the occasional, lonely car passed him by. A colleague told him about a shortcut to the train station that took him through a nearby woodland.

The woods weren't especially large but was home to plenty of tall trees and a few cabins along the side of the road wherein he could see lights and occasionally hear the sounds of life coming from within. He began fantasizing about his own flat, and how comfortable it would be once he arrived and allowed himself to unwind and relax. His daydreaming was led to an abrupt end when he noticed something strange peering out from behind the tree line. He looked over quickly and saw a shadowy figure just as it slipped away back behind the trees.

He thought it was strange that he wasn't able to make out its form, almost like it was a blurry picture in real life. However, he merely rationalized to himself that it must have been some kind of wildlife that he didn't get a good look at because it was dark. He was already tired, so it must have simply been his eyes playing tricks on him. The rest of his walk was markedly uneventful, but he still kept his eyes glued to the trees with a subtle anxiety that the mysterious figure might reappear.

Eventually, he saw the iridescent lights of the train station cutting through the darkness. Markus let out a heavy sigh of relief and redoubled his tempo towards the station. Strangely he noted that a light fog was beginning to set in around him despite the fact that the night had been otherwise totally clear. Nevertheless, he hurried onward as the mist began to encroach upon him.

Just as the haze became so dense that one could no longer see through it, Markus made his way into the station. He stood at the entrance for a second to take in his surroundings now that his vision was no longer obscured. The station was deceptively large with two long platforms running parallel down the center of two sets of tracks. Between the platforms was a covered shelter where the ticket machine was located. He began making his way over to purchase his ticket and passed by a young teenager, average looking for his age with short, styled blonde hair wearing a white hoodie, skinny jeans, checkered canvas sneakers and a face mask. He had his headphones in and was looking intently at his phone. Markus could faintly hear his music as he passed by, but neither acknowledged the other.

Opposite the young man, was a plump, older man sitting with a small book in hands. He was also wearing a face mask which did not fully cover his bushy, white beard, a tartan flat hat, an overcoat, suit trousers, and remarkably clean black oxfords. The older man looked up through his spectacled, hazel eyes and met Markus's gaze; he gave him a polite nod of his head then went back to his book.

The only other person on the platform was a woman around Markus's age, sitting near the ticket machine as he approached. She had a little bit of weight on her, with straight, shoulder-length ginger hair, bright blue eyes, and pale complexion. She wore faded, blue skinny jeans with fashionable tears around the thigh, and a black thin-line top with a denim jacket with violet flower patterns over it.

Having surveyed the scene Markus stood in front of the ticket machine only to find that it was out of service. He let an audible sigh of exasperation and took out his phone to purchase one through his mobile app. However, as he did, he was met with an error saying that phone could not connect to the internet, despite the fact that he had signal. He tried again, and again, and each time to no avail. He decided that he would try his luck again once the train arrived, hoping the conductor would take pity on him given the circumstances, so he grabbed a seat near the woman and waited.

He looked out into the platform outside of the shelter where he was sitting and noticed that the dense fog had made its way into the station where it hung ominously. Several minutes passed in silence, until finally Markus broke the silence to ask the woman about the trains.

"Have you been here for a while? Have you heard or seen any of the trains to Edinburgh?" He asked with a tinge of annoyance in his voice. She looked at him and answered.

"I've been here for twenty minutes; there was an announcement right before you showed up that the train to Edinburgh is getting delayed. But that's all I've heard. The older guy over there told me that he's been waiting for over an hour! The train system in Scotland is shit." She replied with a small chuckle.

Just as quiet began to creep back into the station, the young teen's phone went off startling everyone else. He answered quickly, and Markus couldn't help but overhear.

"Hello?... Hello? Is someone there? I'm just getting static." He looked at his phone screen curiously as the vague sounds of a staticky voice came through. He quickly hung up resolving that it must have been a faulty signal or an incorrect dial. Just as he hung up the phone, the electronic notice board in front of Markus began to glitch out with its pictures disappearing and reappearing with missing pixels and the text changing wildly from letters to numbers and vice versa until it finally settled down.

Markus studied it intensely and read "The next train arriving at platform two is the 11:41PM train to-" it cut off after that and then the screen erupted into erratic glitches with a blaring static noise.

Markus jumped to his feet startled and feverishly looked around just to see the other notice boards doing the same thing. He looked over to the woman who was also sitting fully alert, then to the other end of the shelter and saw the young man looking all around, also clearly alarmed. However, he saw the older man carefully put his book into his bag and slowly stand up, seemingly unphased by the deafening sound. Markus watched anxiously as he calmly made his way out of the shelter and into the heavy mist. Several tense seconds passed, then the sound of train horn cut through the oppressive static as a pair of lights became visible through the fog. The static sound instantly stopped, and the notice board screens returned to normal. Four distinct beeps of train doors chimed from the platform, then the sound of the train starting up, and finally the sound of it leaving the station. The three were once again in the embrace of silence. The woman was the first to speak, as she turned to Markus.

"That was rather odd, did you see the train?"

"Well yeah, its lights were right there." Markus said bluntly and slightly bewildered by her question.

"But did you actually see the train itself? I saw the lights, sure, but as odd as it's about to sound, it didn't look they were coming from anything."

"I mean, it's hard to see anything through this fog, isn't it?"

"I guess... But I can see most of the platform up to the tracks. You'd think you'd see more than just its lights."

"Are you suggesting the old guy just walked off the platform? If there was no train, then why hasn't he come back?"

She opened her mouth to answer but found herself without an explanation. Instead, she merely shrugged her shoulders in defeat and cast her gaze back into the obscuring haze.

Markus felt confident in his rebuttal, but at the same time couldn't shake the strange feeling that perhaps she was on to something. The more time that passed, he became more and more unnerved until a familiar sound rang out through the shelter. The teen's phone went off again and once again he answered.

"Hello?... Oh, hey Dad... I was on my way home, just running a little behind... You're here? How'd you know where I was? I didn't think you'd be off work yet... Okay, yeah I'll meet you outside."

The young man hung up and began gathering his belongings, but just before he left, he took one final glance back at Markus and the woman. Markus couldn't help but notice that the young man had a nervous look on his face, as if somehow hoping to find reassurance in the two strangers on the platform.

Markus locked eyes with him for a second before the young man pulled his hood up and stepped out into the mist. Before his footsteps were out of hearing range, there was a sudden barrage of heavy footsteps that exploded out from behind the shelter heading in the same direction that the young man had just disappeared into. Markus tried to see what it was but could not penetrate the fog. Another couple of seconds passed, then he and the woman heard a muffled scream and the sounds of tearing from the opposite end of the platform.

Markus stood up and walked to the edge of the shelter and felt something or someone's stare burn into him from the fog. Thoroughly shaken now, Markus took a seat nearer the woman. "Something is very wrong here." He said in a whisper.

"The time on the notice board hasn't changed. Look, on my phone it says 11:42 and on the board it's been stuck at 11:34 after it stopped wigging out the first time." She replied anxiously.

"Come to think of it, I've never used this station before, I only heard about it from someone at work. I've been in the area for a while and now that I'm thinking of it, it's pretty strange I've never even heard about it."

"That's odd... This is also my first time on this station; I heard about it from a new girl at work who said it was quicker from the office to my flat."

Just as the pieces were beginning to align for them, she felt a buzz from her phone and read over a text before putting her phone down and looking around frantically.

"What's wrong?" Markus asked apprehensively.

"I just got a text saying my taxi is here, but I never phoned for one."

Just as she replied, the lights began to flicker for a moment before they went out, plunging the shelter and the rest of the station into darkness. The two stand up but were unable to find each other in the darkness.

"Hey! Are you there!? Can you hear me!?" Markus shouted out while frantically waving his arms out in front of him, hoping to find her. Then, he sees a light cut through the darkness and illuminate her face as she lifted her phone to her face.

"I'm right here! I just got another message saying my taxi is about to leave, but all the words are jumbled. I'm pretty freaked out... Where are you?" She said with her head on a swivel as her eyes darted around.

Suddenly, Markus feels a pair of massive, leathery hands grab his head and forcefully pull him to the ground. His senses are momentarily disrupted by the painful impact, but as he reopens his eyes he sees as the woman is similarly dragged to the ground and he scrambles to his feet as he hears her start screaming and struggling.

Her phone fell to the ground with its light shining upwards, and Markus catches a momentary glimpse of a massive, shadowy figure right before it disappears again into the shadows taking the woman with it. Her screams become distant and faint until only a wet, tearing noise can be heard from outside of the shelter's boundary. Markus pulls himself back to his feet but is paralyzed with fear. He feels his hands shaking violently and keeps his eyes glued to the only source of light coming from the woman's phone as it lit of the metallic roof of the shelter.

After a few moments of utter dread and suspense, he could see the lights in the station all come back on at once through the haze. Starting with intermittent blinking, before becoming steady. Almost in a step by step fashion before the shelter's lights themselves turned back on. Markus looks around timidly but sees only a large pool of blood on the ground where the woman was standing and a trail leading away down the platform and out into the dense fog. A voice erupted from the speakers over head for the first time that night, it was full of static and feedback with its words completely inaudible until a single phrase breaks through the maelstrom to say. "this train has three carriages-" And then stops completely.

He is once again left in silence, but now he was completely alone. He begins to hyperventilate as gruesome and horrific thoughts run wild in his head. He then begins to look around fearfully, seeing something truly peculiar. Almost as if part of the fog had lifted in the shape of an archway, Markus saw through it clear as day. He saw a train.

Its lights were all on and its doors were open. He looked inwards from the shelter but didn't see anyone else on the train. He was apprehensive about leaving the shelter, but as he glanced around, he caught a glimpse of the bloody pool and realized that nowhere in the station was safe. A sudden urge crossed him as he took a deep breath and made a break for the train.

To his surprise, he made it into the train without any interruption. He climbed aboard and looked outwards just as the doors closed behind him with a chime. He saw nothing save for the fog, then the train began to move slowly. He could hear it's engines rev up as it transitioned into motion He cautiously moved to his side and took a seat where he could see out the window facing onto the platform. He noticed as the train picked up its pace that the fog was starting to rapidly recede, and as seconds passed him by, more and more of the platform was becoming visible to him, especially the further end of it, where the stairs where, which was previously obscured.

As he moved further up to the exit of the platform, he saw a strange shape on the ground. He quickly made out the shape to be the bloody, mangled corpses of the woman and the teen lying on top of each other. Their limbs were torn and twisted, and their torsos were viciously ripped open with their viscera spilled crudely onto the ground. He could no longer make their faces out now that they'd been brutally butchered. Markus became violently ill and vomited all over the floor of the train. Finally, he pulled his head up, and looked once again out the window and up into the night sky, visible for the first time since he left work that night. However, where the moon should have been hanging, there was an odd moving shape.

A monstrous, demonic silhouette twisted and roiled in the sky above him, seemingly looking at him, taking pleasure in his anguish. He could not comprehend what he was witnessing. He felt his mind being pulled apart and shattered as he gazed upon the impossible vision above him. As his senses began to fail him, one by one, he heard the intercom crackle with static before an eerie, electronic voice said,

"THIS TRAIN WILL NOW TERMINATE."

THE END

CASE THREE

THE GREY LADY

THE RHYTHMIC POUNDING of music accompanied by the flashing of bright LED lights rattled through Ben's ears as he pulled the car to a halt in front of a house teeming with life. He looked over to his sister Claire whose face was glowing with anticipation.

"Looks like Maddie's birthday is pretty low-key, huh?" He said sarcastically.

"Oh yeah, just us and the girls reading books and having some tea." She replied with a chuckle.

"You be safe and have a good time, alright?"

"You too. Tell Taylor and the lads that I said hello." She said with a smile as she exited out of the passenger side.

Ben nodded and waved goodbye to her as she was quickly rushed by a group of her friends.

He saw their mouths moving but could not make out the words for the cacophonous music. He smiled to himself as he pulled away knowing that they were both in for a good night with friends. As he exited the town, he found the drive suddenly very lonesome without the company of his sister.

He turned the radio on and switched rapidly through the stations, dissatisfied with the musical choices of the evening before settling on something bearable. To him, it was much preferable to sitting in silence.

With the sun now totally absent from the sky, he felt claustrophobic as he drove through winding, black roads encroached upon on either side by towering trees. Through their imposing outlines he saw little signs of life save for an occasional small cottage with dim lights which were quickly extinguished by the suffocating darkness that surrounded him. Becoming more and more uneasy, he flicked his car's lights to full and continued down the unending path before him.

Several minutes passed before his radio began to suffer from a sharp staticky interference. He peeled his eyes away from the road to fiddle with it hoping to find something clearer and more palatable. Yet, as he did, something caught his attention from the corner of his eye. He quickly looked back up to see a tall silhouette standing motionless in the middle of the road and in a desperate panicked motion he jerked the car to the side while slamming on the breaks, feeling it tug and twist as it skidded to a halt right before he made contact with the

51

shadow. However, just before the figure came into focus, the jolt of the car's halt whipped Ben's head forward and as he lifted himself up, he noticed that his headlights had gone out. His twitching hands fumbled as he turned them back on. His hairs stood on end when he realized there was nothing in front of him.

A hesitated for a moment, but with a gust of courage, pulled himself from the vehicle with his phone's light illuminating the scene. As he rounded in front of the car, he saw no signs of anything. There were no tracks in the gravel and no indication that anything aside from a few sparse cars had been down this road in quite some time. He swallowed a lump in his throat as the silence and stillness of the scene began to unnerve him. He swung his light around hoping to catch a glimpse of some kind of animal scurrying off into the woods so that he could explain what he saw, but the darkness began to twist his psyche as he slowly backed up to the car where dull, static bellowed ominously from his radio.

Before he could enter the sanctuary of his car, he was met with a start as his phone's ringtone erupted, shattering the silence. He looked down and saw and saw Taylor's name illuminated along with the unmistakable icon of several missed calls. He answered quickly but heard only static for a few moments before a weak crackly voice came through.

"Ben? You there?" Said the voice of his friend Taylor.

"Taylor!? Can you hear me?" Ben said in a panic.

"Fucking hell, mate, your signal is shit."

"Yeah, sorry about that. I just dropped Claire off and I'm in the middle of nowhere."

"Yeah, I saw her post on Facebook. You almost here? We've been waiting for ages."

"I don't know, man. I took some backroads near Shottskirk and now I have no idea where I am."

"Shottskirk? Christ, mate, that's miles away." He paused for a moment before going on. "You good? You sound a little strung out."

"I saw some weird shit. Looked like a person in the middle of the road and I almost hit it but when I stopped to look, I didn't see any sign of anything out here. And now I feel like I'm being watched." He said as he scanned the tree line once again, seeing nothing except for the gentle sway of branches in the wind.

"You had a few?"

"Nah, mate nothing. Anyway, I'll let you know when I'm almost there, you guys go ahead and get started without me, I'll catch up."

"Right, well, hopefully we see you soon. Drive safe, man." And with that, the call ended.

Ben suddenly felt something cold on his neck. Then on his hand. As he looked up, he felt drop by drop as it began to rain on him as dark clouds coalesced overhead. He quickly got back into his car and took one final look through the windshield as the wipers went side to side. He could not shake the eerie feeling of eyes crawling over him, examining his every movement with a burning intensity.

He twisted his head all around looking out of every window hoping that he might something that would alleviate his tension but the fact that he was utterly alone made his skin crawl. As he looked forward, he saw something move from the corner of his eye. It was vague and indescribable, but something had just moved out of sight. Yet, before he could investigate further his car lights flickered before the engine died without warning or explanation.

Ben used his phones light to look around and after a few tense minutes of fiddling with it, the car jumped back to life with the radio playing a low static over a country singer's voice. Now thoroughly disturbed, Ben redoubled himself and sped forward into the night as the rain obscured his vision.

Nearly half an hour went by without any other strange occurrences, yet he could not escape the haunting feeling of being watched. A bolt of lightning and a crack of booming thunder rang out and briefly illuminated a building on his side as he was approaching it. The towering crucifix at its apex indicated it was a church, yet its architecture was archaic. It was likely a relic dating back to the Victorian era, complete with a sprawling graveyard lined with row upon row of faded and cracked headstones. With his eyes glued to it examining its structure, he was unable to notice the massive flooded puddle as he careened into it, causing the car to begin hydroplaning across the jagged stone road. As he corrected the car and brought it to a stop, once again the headlights flickered before going out completely along with the engine.

Ben huffed an exasperated breath as he began to apply the fixes that had worked before. Yet, to his dismay, this time they were of no avail. The car was thoroughly dead. He checked his phone, preparing to dial for assistance but noticed that his battery was nearly dead. This struck him as especially odd considering it had been nearly fully charged when he answered Taylor's call. Had his flashlight drained the battery that much? Ben pondered to himself; it seemed impossible, but he refused to introspect any further fearing any further implications.

He rested his head on the steering wheel for a moment to collect himself. As he began to catch his breath, he looked out of his side window at the church and once again caught a chilling sight. The church had some low lights positioned upwards to illuminate it, but they cast a strange shadow that Ben could not look away from. Lights cast from the graveyard created a looming shadow on the broad side of the church's stone walls. Ben looked intensely at it and made out its shape to be that of a human wearing some long, flowy garb. He shook it off after a minute. It had not moved at all, so it must have been an oddly shaped branch or a statue casting a shadow. After all, why would anyone be out in the middle of a storm in the middle of nowhere?

Brushing it off as paranoia, he looked out of the other side of his vehicle and saw a large sign that was dimly lit by a series of lamps. It read "Welcome to the Grey Hills". The rest of the sign's words were scratched and illegible, but Ben found it odd he'd never even heard of it. He lifted himself up and noticed something else, something that brought about a wave of relief. Over the hill and through the forest, he saw lights. Finally, civilization, he thought as he quickly gathered what belongings he could carry with him and pushed open his door, throwing caution to the wind. He locked the car automatically with his key and he made his pilgrimage towards the light with the rain now beating down on him.

Steep, muddy ravines and angular hills served as his adversary as he trudged through the woods. He felt bramble grabbing and cutting him as he pushed past with jagged and sharp rocks causing his feet to ache through his shoes now coated with thick layers of mud. Then once again the feeling returned. He felt eyes burning holes into his back. He stopped for a minute to look around. However, while he might have expected to see nothing, this time he was met with his pursuers.

Several shadowy figured stood menacingly in the distance. His blood ran cold with fear, but he knew he past the point of no return and picked up his pace as he dashed through the treacherous night, hoping to escape them. With every step he exhaled and inhaled sharply, as panicked breaths left his body. Around every corner he saw them watching him motionlessly. Their features were indistinct, but Ben took no time to stop and examine them. His intuition told him that if he stopped for even a moment, it would be the last thing he'd ever do. So, he raced through the woods with their indescribable malice eating away at him as they appeared before him at every step.

Finally, he reached a clearing and broke free of the shadowy boughs of the forest and saw the source of the light he had seen faintly from the church. An old, seemingly derelict mansion stood among overgrown grass with a brilliant light peering through the main window. As he approached, he tripped when his foot hit a large, upturned root and he looked back to see them all standing at the forest's edge. Their eyes were invisible to Ben, but he felt their gaze stabbing into him like dozens of knives. In a last, desperate struggle he lifted himself up and bolted for the front door of the house.

He slammed on the front door begging and pleading for whomever was inside to let him in. He peered back towards the woods but saw nothing. It filled him with dread to not know their whereabouts now that they'd made themselves seen. Fed up with waiting, Ben grabbed hold of the doorknob and thrust into it, finding it to be unlocked. Then as he burst through the door, he quickly turned on his heel and shut the door behind and locked it. He took a step back to examine the door, as if he were waiting for something to violently slam into to, but for all his anxieties, nothing happened. The gentle patter of rain on glass and the creaking of the house's old bones were his only company.

However, despite his serene surroundings, he felt even more uneasy than he had before. He turned around to face into the home and looked to see the radiant glow that had lured him in peeking out from the far corner of the house. He called out a meek hello with a quiver in his voice. Just as he had done so, the light suddenly extinguished. However, with no more options, he ventured further in to investigate.

With every footstep against the ancient wood floorboards, his heart raced. After walking past the seemingly endless hallway, he turned the corner to find a massive parlor room where a fireplace had just been doused. His eyes danced around the room examining photo frames too coated in dust and cobwebs to make out their subjects.

Opposite the fireplace hang a large mirror which seemed to draw Ben towards it. As he approached, he saw something that made his skin crawl. Within the mirror's reflection, he saw a figure sitting in the armchair in front of the fireplace. He had not noticed it since its back was to him when he entered, but now it was clear that he was not alone in the house.

He swallowed the lump in his throat and approached the figure slowly. He made out that it was a woman's figure, judging by its slight frame, but oddly, she was slouched over to her side. He felt an intense wave of dread the closer he got until he felt his feet glued to the floor unable to move at all. With a last gambit he called out to her.

"Hello?" He meekly cried.

She then began to shudder in place as her body began to stiffen up. Slowly and inhumanly, she righted her posture until she was seated perfectly upright. The pounding of Ben's heart made his eardrums swell. Accompanied by the tapping of rain on glass, the woman stood up with her back to him. Then, she turned to face him as if spun in place.

Ben's blood ran cold as her side profile gave way to her front facing position. What he was horrible and
left his sensibilities in retreat.

Where her face would have been was shredded and torn with thick gooey ribbons of blood and sinew exposing a stained skull with milky white eyes seated in two bloody sockets. Her long, tangled hair curled over matted with blood and bits of flesh. Her ancient looking dress was torn and coated with mud and debris which betrayed the fact that beneath them, there were no legs. She simply floated in place with her horrifying eyes burning into Ben's.

She began to float around the chair towards him and when she was within mere inches of him, he was granted a divine boon and given the wits to turn and make his escape. He made it to the end of the hallway and struggled to unlock the door, and as he did, he turned back to see her floating out from behind and heading straight for him.

Finally, he was able to free the lock and with that, he burst through the door and with inhuman speed dashed back through the forest. With the path somewhat familiar to him now, and with the supernatural fear of what he had witnessed he made short work of his trek back through the woods. However, as he was crossing a particularly steep slope, he slipped on its muddy wall and crashed down onto a pile of jagged rock leaving his knee with a searing gash.

He screamed out in agony and pulled himself to a seated upright position to examine his knee. As he did so, a crash of lightning illuminated the sky and once again he saw the shadowy figures that had chased him through the woods once again. In the moment of lighting, he saw them all standing above him just over the top of the hill staring down at him with pale, glowing white eyes. He gasped in horror and pulled himself to his feet to make his escape.

Despite the injury to his knee, he made his way out of the woods without any further incident. Time seemed to pass him by at an extraordinary pace. While he felt like it taken him an eternity to get through those damnable woods, it now seemed like he had blinked and before he knew it he had raced past the church where his defunct car had initially broken down.

Finally running out of steam, and with his knee now past its capacity to move, he leaned up against his car and tried to catch his breath. After several long, sputtering inhalations he felt the sensation of a burning glare digging deep into his back. He whipped his head around and saw a congregation of the shadow figures all crowded around the faceless woman watching him from the corner of the forests edge. Unable to keep running he tightly closed his eyes, praying that whatever happened next would be painless. But as moments passed, he felt nothing. No grasp of cold, otherworldly hands. Nothing.

He slowly opened his eyes and saw that they had disappeared. A wave of relief washed over him but was short lived. A strange stinging sensation burrowed deep into the back of his hand. He lifted it up to his face to examine it and saw a strange mark etched into his flesh. It was familiar, though he was unsure why, as he was sure he'd never seen it before.

The rain overhead began to dissipate, and Ben slowly staggered his way back down the road hoping to come across the small convenience store he had passed on his way in. The road was empty now save for the howling of wind rustling through the trees. Ben was relieved however, as he no longer felt the digging of eyes into him. For the first time that evening, he finally felt safe.

His shoes had carried him for a mile before the glowing sign of the store cut through the darkness of the night. He cautiously entered and met the eyes of the clerk. He struggled to catch his breath as he hobbled over.

"Seen the woman in grey?" He asked gruffly, catch Ben off-guard.

The terror and shock on Ben's face must have been a satisfactory reply as the man went on.

"You're lucky. Most people who go through those woods don't come back. I've heard of few that did, but they ended up finishing the job themselves."

"What are you going on about? What the fuck was all that?" Ben huffed.

"People say that if you encounter her, she doesn't leave you. Haunts 'me. Pokes at them from the shadows until they go mad. Folks around here call her the Grey Lady. Decades ago, a wealthy mining family got into some financial trouble. Apparently, the husband took to the drink and one night he went too far with her, abusing and shaming her until she left in the family car in the dead of night, in the middle of a nasty storm and ended up in a ditch with her face all torn up. Except she wasn't dead. It's said that she pulled herself up and dragged herself to the abandoned house in the woods where she died, leaving behind a foul curse on the land.

Her husband apparently followed her trail in the morning when she didn't come home and found her torn up body in the armchair of the house. Shot himself in the parlor room of their house a few days later. Now, she leaves the lights on in the house, calling in

60

unlucky people who mysteriously break down by the church. You're lucky to be here. Come sit down and I'll call you a Taxi."

Ben stood in shock and disbelief at the tale he had been told. The mark on his hand began to ignite with pain as the clerk walked into the backroom. He wandered to the front of the store to look out through the large window and felt his heart drop. From across the street, he saw her standing there motionless. Her pale, white eyes locked onto him as his vision began to fade in and out. He prayed that he would blink, and she would be gone. But as he closed and reopened his eyes, he saw her surrounded by the shadow figures once again. Without another moment, **HE COLLAPSED TO THE FLOOR.**

CASE FOUR

Somethings Outside

FROM AN EXTERIOR VIEW, one would not be able to make out the conversation happening between the occupants of the rusty, bumbling van cruising down the gravelly pathway into Autumn's Creek. However, from inside, Ross McGhee and Emily Sharpe were in the heat of a brutal argument. While the couple was generally very warm and loving, Emily could not help but feel a disconnect between them and as evidenced by their bickering, tensions were beginning to rise. Their squabbling came to an abrupt halt when Ross looked forward away from Emily and suddenly slammed on the brakes while tightening his muscles.

The pair were jolted forward, knocking the wind from them. Emily whipped her head up furiously, ready to barrage Ross for his sudden brake, but then saw as a small deer stood frozen before them. The pair stare at the creature for a few moments before it gathered the courage to continue down its path before disappearing into the woods.

The drive was silent after they resumed down the trail. Eventually they passed a sign made of rotten wood reading "Welcome to Autumn's Creek!" along with a cartoonish buck in a forest ranger's outfit.

"Can you stop up there at that convenience store? I really need to use the bathroom." Emily finally said, breaking the silent tension.

"Yeah, I could go for a smoke, anyway." Ross replied quietly, trying to inflect a less confrontational tone than the one he had been using earlier.

As they pulled up, Ross put the van in park and shut off the engine as Emily darted out of the passenger side headed towards the store's entrance. With his fiancé out of sight, Ross let out an exasperated sigh as he too stepped out of the vehicle. He walked a few yards down a hill so he was facing out into the expansive forest that Autumn's Creek was known for. He smacked the bottom of a pack of cigarettes he held in his breast pocket before pulling one out and lighting it. Just as he pulled the first drag, he heard an earsplitting screech echo out from deep within the forest. However, it was brief and followed quickly by silence.

"Ross!" Emily called out from behind him.

"What's up?" He had nonchalantly before taking another puff.

"There was no one in there. Like, not even a shopkeeper, and the store was completely ransacked."

"Oh," Ross replied with a furled brow. "that's really strange."

"Do you think we should try calling the police?"

"I don't think it's really our issue. There's lots of wildlife out here it might have been a bear or something. I just heard a crazy screech from deep in the woods, so maybe that's your culprit. Besides, I don't even have signal out here."

"I don't know…" Emily trailed off. "I don't like it though; can we please just get back to the van and get out of here?"

Ross nodded as he took a final drag of his cigarette before tossing it to the ground and stomping it out with his boot. The pair then quickly hiked back to the van and got back on the main road heading towards the bungalow they'd be staying at for the weekend. As they drove away, Emily continued to look at the abandoned store with an uneasy feeling that something nefarious had happened.

The sun was falling slightly past its zenith heralding the sweltering heat of the afternoon as the pair turned past the bend placing the bungalow directly into their line of sight. The two floored structure stood proudly with its oaken frame surrounded on its sides with beautiful plants and well-kept brush. However, something was instantly amiss to Emily as they slowed the van to a halt.

"Ross the front door is wide open." She said with a serious tone.

He had an intense look on his face as he surveyed the scene. "Wait here, I'm going to go look inside."

She didn't want to see him go in alone, but she found herself unnerved after what she had witnessed in the abandoned shop. Ross made his way up the small staircase to the front porch. He paused before he entered and looked in through the adjacent window but made no movements to indicate any concern. Then he cautiously stepped inside and disappeared behind the door frame as he rounded the corner.

Emily waited for several agonizing minutes, praying that he would just come back out and tell her everything was clear. Then she heard a muffled yelp of horror echo out from the house as Ross burst back through the front entrance before doubling over the side of the railing and letting loose a torrent of vomit.

Emily quickly erupted from the passenger's seat with a feeling of panic, that Ross could see from where he was standing.

"There's a fucking dead deer in the living room!" He cried out with strands of spit and vomit on his lips.

"What!?" Emily echoed as she started making her way over to him.

"Stop! Don't get any closer, the smell is absolutely vulgar and it's a bloody mess inside."

"So, what am I supposed to do, just wait in the car!?"

"Just give me a damn minute to collect myself and get this thing out of here!" He barked back.

Emily huffed an exasperated sigh as she tossed her hands to the side, clearly frustrated with his response. Ross went back inside to re-examine the grisly scene. He stepped into the room with his shirt pulled up over his nose to help mitigate the foul odor. He traced the outline of the deer sprawled out with its guts spilled out onto the floor and its throat slit.

He noticed that the deer wasn't particularly large, so he felt confident that he could drag it out by himself. Strangely he noticed for as gruesome as the scene was, there was very little blood, as if it had been killed somewhere and brought here, and the rest of the house was in pristine condition.

While the whole scene didn't sit right with him, he decided that it was probably explainable and simply rationalized that maybe a some larger animal had dragged it here to eat it later, and that the front door must have been accidentally left open by the owners before Ross and Emily arrived. He didn't want to explore the possibilities and play crime scene investigator any longer so he grabbed the carcass by its feet and began to pull it outside where he would load it on a tarp in the van and drop the corpse off somewhere far away so as not to invite the company of any dangerous wildlife.

Emily gagged when she saw him dragging the deer out but steeled her nerves and helped him carry it to the van and load it up. The pair then drove out the brushes near the forest's entry and they deposited it there, promising to phone the forest rangers later and inform them so they could handle it.

They exchanged few words outside of the disbelief and shock of what had happened as they drove back to the cabin. They were both thankful that between the two of them the cleanup took little time, and before they knew it the house was back to its picturesque condition.

"Care to join me on a hike before it gets too dark?" Emily asked as affixed her beanie over her short brown hair.

"Definitely. I've got this little game camera that I want to set up so we can keep an eye on the place in case anymore hungry beasts want to show up."

As they closed the door behind them, Ross placed the camera on its fixture on the front porch so that it could get a long view of the front yard of the bungalow and face out into the forest that stood around the perimeter.

As the pair ventured through the scenic trail accompanied by the babbling of a nearby brook as they stumbled upon an ancient looking well overgrown with moss and vines on the top of a hill.

"Think it's a wishing well?" Emily asked coyly as she quickened her pace towards it.

"If it is, maybe we can wish for no more weird things out here." Ross chimed back.

Emily looked inside but dropped her shoulders and let out a disappointed sigh when she saw that it was totally empty save for the growth of mold and a few plants.

"I think I'd rather have wished to know what's been going on with you lately." She said in a more somber tone.

"I'm fine…" Ross said trailing off.

"You're obviously not. You've been so irritable and argumentative, and even sometimes just downright mean. Why do you keep pushing me away when this whole trip was supposed to be so that we'd be closer?" She felt herself fighting back tears as she let out her inner thoughts.

"Things have just been hard to deal with lately… I don't think the antidepressants have been doing much for me lately." He whispered. "I didn't want to worry you, so I didn't mention it. I'm sorry for acting like such a bastard."

She quickly dashed over to him and wrapped her arms around his waist and pulled him in close. "Your battle is my battle, no matter what."

He embraced her back and squeezed tight, feeling the weight begin to lift from his chest now that he was finally allowing his defenses to fall. Their tender moment shattered as soon as they heard rustling and voices approaching from the opposite end of the wood.

They kept their eyes glued to the tree line as a group of four teenagers carrying sound equipment and cameras appeared.

"Oh, hi!" The leader of the group called out.

"Uh, hello?" Emily echoed reluctantly.

"I hope we aren't interrupting anything; we're shooting a documentary out here. Would you guys mind answering a few questions?"

"I suppose not." Ross muttered taken aback by their rude supposition.

"Fantastic." The leader said as she handed some equipment over to the larger young man to her side. "Are you familiar with the legend of the Autumn's Creek Huntsman?" She said holding a secondhand microphone up to the pair while the other three of her group held up cameras and a boom microphone behind her.

"No," Ross began, "what's that?"

"You guys aren't locals?" She asked expectantly.

"No, we're renting a cabin and just staying for the weekend." Emily replied sternly.

She let out an exasperated sigh as she quickly began to scurry away from them, clearly dissatisfied with the interview. The other three quickly began to pack their belongings and follow after her without a single word. Ross and Emily simply shot each other a look of bewilderment at the strange ordeal. However, they simply shrugged their shoulders and wrote them off as eccentric locals. With the sun now getting lower behind the trees, they turned their heels and made their way back to the cabin, hand in hand.

With visions of the morning's various plans fresh in their heads, for the first time in what felt like ages the two finally felt excited to be together. Emily looked up at the clock and yawned.

"Jesus, it's already 9:30. We should probably get ready for bed. Thanks again for making dinner, babe. I'll get the dishes put away and meet you upstairs in a minute okay?" Emily said as she picked up their plates, planting a kiss on the top of Ross's head.

A smile crept over his face as he stood up and made his ascent up the stairs. As Emily was nearly finished with the dishes, excited to spend a night alone with her fiancé, she heard a blood-curdling scream from outside, quickly followed by another even louder shriek. The first sounded like a girl's voice, but the other did not even sound human. The sudden shock caused Emily to drop the plate she was holding into the sink with a loud crash. She peered outside and through the darkness she could see motion as the branches swayed against the breeze as something passed through them.

Thoroughly startled, she quickly headed upstairs to find Ross seated in the bed facing the television. She scanned the room and saw his laptop set up on the desk at the far end of the room. Without a word she stormed over to it and began fiddling around on it.

"What's up?" Ross asked quizzically.

"Can you pull up the feed from that camera you set up outside?" She asked with a serious tone. "I heard something really weird outside and I saw something massive moving around near the trees."

Ross guided her hand and had her pull up the footage from the camera which had apparently gone off several times throughout the day since their arrival. Nothing was of particular interest as the motion sensor had been set off mostly by squirrels, passing birds, and the occasional deer. But then, they saw something peculiar.

Four figures had been captured skulking around the property not long after their arrival. Ross and Emily were instantly able to identify them as the young filmmakers they had encountered earlier.

"Think they had anything to do with that deer we found when we got here?" Ross asked with a tone of unease. "Maybe they were trying to fake some footage for whatever local legends they were talking about?"

"Maybe." Emily mused. "I doubt it though. They were weird but they didn't really seem like the type to do anything as dramatic as that."

She let out a distressed sigh and hung her head in her hands. "I heard something weird outside before I came up here. Sounded like a girl and something weird... definitely not like any animal I had ever heard before."

"Probably just those kids scaring each other out in the woods in pursuit of the deadly Huntsman of Autumn's Creek!" Ross teased as he grabbed her sides and began tickling Emily, making growling sounds as he did.

"Cut it out!" She squealed between fits of laughter and spasms. "Let's just get to bed so we're not too exhausted tomorrow morning."

Several minutes passed and the two of them were comfortably positioned in bed, feeling the tingling of sleep which made their eyelids heavy. Their serene scene was suddenly interrupted as a deafening screech broke though the silence. Without a moment's hesitation Ross jumped out of bed and threw on some pants and a jacket and trudged downstairs to investigate the cause of the disturbance. He threw open the door and shined his flashlight along the perimeter that was visible from the front door. The site was still except for the eeriness of it. The sound echoed through his mind, and it bore an uncanny resemblance to the cry he had heard earlier that morning at the convenience store.

From the bedroom window. Emily looked out and once again saw unexplainable movement as something large and fast dashed through the forest surrounding them. She jolted out of bed and examined the live feed of the camera and saw as Ross was positioning it back in its original place after it had been apparently knocked loose. She let out an audible gasp of terror as she saw from behind him with his back to the woods as something began to emerge from the shadows. She ran to the stairs and screamed out for Ross.

"Get back! Something's outside!"

Curiosity gripped Ross and compelled him to face the mysterious figure. He whipped around and when he saw it, his skin went pale and he stumbled backwards in fright and disbelief. The creature approached the house where the lights made its features clear. It was impossibly large with pale, leathery skin. From its backside several long appendages jutted out with multiple articulated joints. Its front side was long and vaguely humanoid with two shorter limbs outstretched with jagged points at its tips. Its head was insectoid with two black holes for eyes and powerful mandibles lined with rows of pointed teeth. And in its terrible mandible it held the bloodied, massacred remains of the lead documentarian with her limbs broken and shredded and her innards dangling as it approached.

Ross rushed through the entryway and slammed the door behind him and locked it before he ran upstairs to be with Emily. From the camera's stream on the laptop, they watched fighting back the desire to faint or be nauseous as the creature began to furiously dig at a point in the yard. It took the monster little time to uncover the earth to reveal a massive burial ground nearly overflowing with bones and decaying flesh.

No longer able to cope with the horrors she was witnessing, Emily let loose a scream as she began to back away from the screen. Ross quickly ran back to try to comfort her but could not bring himself to take his eyes away from the carnage outside. From the camera's stream, he watched as the beast dropped the mangled body of the young lady in with the other remains before it stood on its hind legs and outstretched its body to its full height, easily towering over the trees behind it.

It let out a blood chilling screech as it began move towards the house beckoned by Emily's cries. Ross knew they needed to move, so he helped Emily back up to her feet and pulled her into the hallway. He heard the creature beating at the front door trying to gain entrance. His eyes darted around looking for an escape route and just as the door began to splinter, he saw the hatch that led up to the loft above them. With Emily's help the two pulled the ladder down and made their ascent just as the door gave way to the monster's unnatural strength.

They quickly pulled the ladder up with them and shut the hatch before positioning themselves in the corner struggling to not make any noise. Below them, they could only listen helplessly as the creature skittered throughout the house. Despite its massive size, it somehow moved silently with the only audible sounds it was making being a low clicking noise as it moved throughout the floors.

Eventually the noise stopped directly below them, and they muffled their mouths as they heard it begin to make an excited hissing and growling sound. Then it began to bash violently against the loft's floor until it broke through with one of its jagged elongated hands.

Emily and Ross could only hope to suppress their screams as they watched it blindly reach around mere inches away from them.

Just as all hope seemed lost, they heard a new sound from outside the house. The creature noticed as well, as it ceased its onslaught. Emily and Ross began to loosen up their tense muscles as the listened for the beast hearing it rush across the road chasing after the distressed cries of some unfortunate soul who must have heard the commotion then stumbled across the monster's burial site. Then the screams were silent.

Without a moment to spare, Emily and Ross picked themselves up and made a mad dash down and out of the house towards the van parked outside. As Ross fumbled with the keys. Emily cried out in horror as the beast descended once again from the neighboring trees with its freshest victim spattering blood and viscera. Suddenly the car came to life and the pair raced out around the monster and back the way they had come earlier in the day.

Ross pressed the pedal down as hard as he could, pressing the van to pierce through the night with their pursuer closing in on them. Yet, as they approached the end of the forest where the sign read "Welcome to Autumn's Creek!" The creature suddenly ceased its advance and darted off to the side and into the veil of the trees.

Emily and Ross took a long look at one another before repositioning themselves facing forward. From that day forward, they would refuse to discuss any of the horrifying events that occurred at Autumn's Creek.

The End

CASE FIVE

THE OTHER

AS THE SUN SET painting the October sky in brilliant orange, red, and pink hues, a young woman was nearly home as her taxi carefully rounded a corner. With her head pressed lightly against the window, she looked out longingly, daydreaming about the night to come. Once she felt the soft vibrations of her phone, she lifted herself up and rifled through the bag she had placed next to her. Without checking to see who was calling, and saw her friend, Jason's name appears she immediately answers the call.

"Hello?" She answered nonchalantly.

"Hey, Olivia! Are we all still down for tonight?" He replied excitedly.

"Of course!" She answered spritely. "It's all I could think about all day, work was an absolute drag today, but I'm so ready to cut loose."

"Hell yeah, it's going to be awesome."

"I've got all my parents' cheesy slasher films lined up and enough liquor to get everyone messed up."

"Sweet, I've got my own collection of alcohol I'm bringing too. I think everyone's going to be absolutely dead by tomorrow morning." He laughed. "Oh, and I've got some really creepy games we can all play when it gets late that way no one has to worry about getting any restful sleep."

"Fantastic, I wouldn't want it any other way." She said excitedly.

"Have you heard from Marc yet?"

"Radio silence."

"Same here. I'll call him in a second to let him know we're all still getting together. Later!"

"Cool, then I'll see you guys soon. Later." She answered in the affirmatory.

She looked up and caught the taxi driver looking at her in the rear-view. She caught her own reflection and noticed her long, ginger hair was pushed aside in a way she hated to see.

"Which street am I looking for, miss?" He asked shyly.

"Adelaide Street, thank you." She responded as she fixed her hair and readjusted her glasses comfortably on her face.

He nodded and turned his attention back to the road before him. Olivia turned back to face out the window. She watched as the extravagant, two-floor houses appeared and disappeared from her view as they sped down the road. Olivia always felt somewhat self-conscious about the fact that her family lived in such a lavish neighborhood. Growing up, most of her friends and classmates would call her the "rich girl". It wasn't a title she was proud of, considering it was her parents' success and not her own. She herself preferred to present herself more humbly. Yet still, she could not deny the fact that lived a charmed life.

After a few minutes, the taxi slowed to a halt as they pulled into the driveway of the Morris estate. From base to roof, the entire house was meticulously bedecked with Halloween flair. Plastic skeletons peered through windows as massive spiders crept around a minefield of fake tombstones. At the front door, an enormous grim reaper animatronic stood menacingly amidst a cloud of low-lying fog with glowing green LED eyes. Even from within the taxi, she could hear the cackling of witches coming from the ambient soundtrack being played from the loudspeakers. She saw as a group of young children ran up past the taxi to the front door where they were greeted by Olivia's mother who was handing out candy to the young trick-or-treaters before returning back inside.

"Here we are, your fare comes out to £4:65." The driver said matter-of-factly.

Olivia reached into her purse as she gathered her belongings, she pulled a five-pound note loose and presented it the man. "Don't worry about the change. Have a nice evening!"

"Thank you very much, ma'am. You have a good one, too."

As she exited, she began to walk up to the front door as the driver pulled away. She took a deep breath as she stood at the threshold. While she had mixed feelings about indulging in her parents' wealth, she was always excited for the holiday seasons, considering they always went full salvo. It was better than if they were just two stuck up old folks who spent their holidays tucked away inside counting their coins.

As she pressed through the front door, she was greeted by her father dressed in an elaborate priest costume.

"Olivia! How was work, sweetheart?" He asked excitedly.

"Oh, it was fine. I'm only glad it's over. You and mom getting ready to head out soon?" She could tell he'd already had quite a bit to drink. She struggled to hide a smile as she watched him clumsily meander around.

"Yes, we are." Her mother called from the living room. "Though, I think this one will probably not even make it to the function before passing out."

Her mother emerged in an equally impressive nun outfit to match with her husband. It was cute that they always matched, Olivia thought.

"Oh, Olivia, dinner is ready and in the microwave for you and your friends." She said as she came up to Olivia and put her into a loving hug.

"Thanks, mum."

"I wish we could stay a little longer, but we're going to be late." She said as she released Olivia.

"No worries. Are you guys staying over there tonight?"

Her mother looked over at her father. "More than likely." She said with a chuckle.

Her father came in quickly and throw his arms around them both. "Have a great night, sweetie. Love you, bunches." He said as Olivia's mother began shuffling him out.

"Love you guys too. See you tomorrow!"

Olivia cracked open a bottle of water from the fridge as she heard the front door click shut, and suddenly she realized she was alone. After finishing a few thirst-quenching sips, she made her way upstairs past fake cobwebs and plastic pumpkins with permanent expressions of horror and mischief. Once at her door she threw it open and quickly stepped inside with the dull, echoey sound of Halloween ambiance at her back.

She took a deep breath as she looked around her room. Its black and red abstract color scheme adorned the walls as she walked up to her double bed where she dropped her bag with a heavy thud that caused the springs to recoil. She heard the unmistakable sound of a children shrieking in delight come from outside her house and she paced over to her large window to look out at the commotion. She felt a smile creep across her face as she saw scores of children running around with their costumes. The season always brought warm feelings of nostalgia as she recalled her own adventures with her friends back when they would partake in the holiday's festivities.

After a moment, she turned on her heels and made her way out of the room to take a shower in the bathroom adjacent from the hallway that her room was located on. As she stepped past the room's frame, the lights above her and throughout the house began to violently flicker before returned to normal.

She let out a gasp when it happened and found herself frozen. Once she was convinced that the power would not fail her, she let out a sigh of relief. Satisfied believing that the fluctuations must have simply been due to the amount of power consumed by all the lights and fixtures, Olivia completed her shower without interruption before returning to her room to get ready for the party to come.

Just as soon as she entered into the room, her phone erupted with its ringtone causing her to jump with a start. She grabbed her phone from off the bed and noticed that it was an unknown caller. Despite that she answered and heard a familiar voice.

"Olivia! It's Jason."

"Hey! I didn't recognize the number, where are you calling from?"

"It's Marc's new phone. I was playing on it and decided to call you from it so that you'd have each other's numbers. We met up and now we're heading over, we're like, fifteen minutes away."

"Oh, cool, I'll be ready by the time you guys get here. Did you dress up or anything?"

"No, figured we were probably just going to be hanging out, so we didn't really see the point."

"Oh, okay." She replied with more than a little disappointment. "Then I guess I'll see you when you guys get here."

"Yep, see you soon!" Then Jason hung up the phone.

Olivia looked at her ensemble that she had been excited to wear for the event. It wasn't anything particularly ornate, just a few pieces of clothes she had seen at a thrift store that she thought would have made the perfect witch costume. However, she would have felt awkward being the only one to dress up, so instead she changed into more mundane clothes and prepared herself for Jason and Marc's arrival.

She would not have to wait long though; no sooner had she finished setting out the alcohol and snacks, there was a sturdy series of knocks. She rushed over and excitedly threw open the door and was greeted by two imposing figures. They both wore featureless white masks which stood out menacingly against their dark, hooded jackets. Olivia had no time to react before they both lurched forward with a loud roar and hands outstretched. She screamed and tripped backwards before being assailed with the sound of their cackling laughter.

The two men at her doorway removed their masks and revealed themselves to be Marc and Jason.

"You assholes!" She exclaimed with a nervous chuckle as she stood herself back up with their help.

"You should have seen the look on your face!" Marc howled between laughs.

Jason finally caught his breath before chiming in. "So where are the drinks? I'm so ready to get absolutely melted."

"In the kitchen, I think we all need a drink after that." Olivia paused for a second when she saw Marc was carrying a large black plastic bag with him. "What's in the bag?"

"Oh, just a little something for us to do when we get bored." Marc answered coyly.

"Oh, so mysterious." Olivia said sarcastically. "Come on, help me bring everything upstairs to the media room. I've already got everything set up."

Roughly two hours passed them by as they exchanged news on the ongoings of their lives, played several rounds of an online zombie survival game along with a few horror simulation games on Jason's recommendation. They had started a bloody slasher movie but found themselves drunkenly talking over it while pointing out how bad the acting and plot were.

"Goddamn, this movie sucks. Would you guys care if I turned it off?" Olivia asked as she staggered to her feet and made her way over to the television.

"Not at all, in fact would you mind killing the lights? I think it's time I break out my special surprise." Marc chimed in as he began rifling through the bag.

"I don't think I've got the wits about me to play a complicated board game." Jason murmured from his seated position.

"Trust me you won't need your wits for this." He said as he pulled out several tall, black candles and began to align them along the ground.

With Jason and Olivia's curious attention, Marc presented what he had been keeping secret. Between the array of candles, he placed down a thin, frayed piece of cardboard along with a strange wooden object with a piece of glass in its center.

"Did you really bring a Ouija board?" Olivia exclaimed in disbelief.

"Yeah I got it from some weird little antique store the other day when I was looking for inspiration for a costume. The shop owner was kind of cagey about it, and he said to 'be careful' with it."

"For good reason, I don't want to mess with that thing." Olivia protested.

"Afraid of ghosts?" Marc mockingly hissed while pantomiming ghostly movements.

"Oh, shut up, Marc, just set it up and we can ask the spirits who the biggest jackass in the room is." Jason replied while lowering himself to his level, placing his index fingers on the planchet.

Olivia hesitated, but yielded and then knelt down besides the boys and placed her fingers into position. The instant her fingers made contact with the small wooden object, the lights all around them began to flicker before completely going out completely.

"Are the lights on a timer or something?" Jason asked nervously.

Before Olivia had the chance to reply, the three felt the planchet quickly dash around the board spelling out the word 'hello'. They all looked at each other anxiously.

"You're scaring us, Marc." Olivia whispered.

"I'm not doing anything..." Marc answered before looking around the room. "Is there anyone here with us?"

The planchet slid over to the top right corner landing squarely on the word 'yes'.

"Alright, Marc, good gag, you got us, man. Now quit it." Jason muttered.

"I swear I'm not doing anything." He looked anxiously at the dial and then continued. "What is your name?"

The planchet then darted around the board once again without hesitation, spelling out the name Valin. Just as it stopped moving, the candles all extinguished themselves one by one. Thoroughly fed up with the phenomena, Olivia told the others it was time to stop, but as she went to pull her hands away from the pointer, it began to move around once again. No return. Olivia. Hold. Pointer. With the last word spelled out, Jason and Marc quickly looked up to Olivia in shock.

"It's not me... I can't feel my arm..." She muttered with a quiver in her voice.

Ask. Question.

"Alright, Valin." Marc began after a moment's hesitation. "What do you want with us?" He asked with a tinge of unease and disbelief.

Olivia grunted in pain as she felt the planchet beneath her fingers becoming hot like burning metal. She tried to pry herself free, but by the hand of some mysterious force was unable to as the planchet moved once again.

P.O.S.S.E.S.I.O.N

Then without warning or explanation, the board and the wooden pointer exploded out from under the group and launched itself at the wall with immense force. Jason and Marc looked back at Olivia in horror as she fell completely flat on her back and began to furiously convulse. Marc lunged forward to steady her and held her face forward. He watched as her eyes rolled to the back of her head with spit and foam pouring from her mouth. Jason leapt to his feet at the sight of the commotion and began to make a break for the door in an attempt to escape.

Jason tightly gripped the doorknob and forcefully pulled and twisted but found himself unable to open the door. He then heard a bloodcurdling scream come from Marc followed by sudden silence. He quickly jerked back around and watched in horror as Marc began to be lifted up into the air by and invisible hand. With a spine-chilling snap, Marc's head was violently spun around to face Jason. He saw the look of fear in Marc's lifeless eyes as blood began to pool out of his mouth and from the corners of his eyes.

Marc's body the hit the floor with a loud thump as he was released by whatever was grasping him. Without a sound, Olivia's body began to rise up in unnatural motions, as if hoisted up by something else. He was unable to speak with his tongue frozen with fright.

Olivia's once bright eyes were now replaced with an eerie, bleak whiteness. She began to speak in tongues, muttering nonsense as she effortlessly floated over towards Jason.

He began to turn around to try the door once again, but before he could, he felt his body become paralyzed as he began to be lifted into the air. He looked at Olivia and watched as her hands mirrored his ascent. With a twist of her hand, his right arm twisted and shattered into pieces. He screamed out in pain as she moved her other hand causing his left arm to be crushed in the same way.

With Jason still suspended in the air, Olivia floated over and upwards towards him until they were face to face. Her pale white eyes momentarily returned to their normal hue and she whimpered out. "I'm sorry". Just as she finished, her eyes turned jet black. Jason looked over from the corner of his eyes to see as the light cast from outside revealed a monstrous form behind Olivia.

"What are you?" Jason asked as he choked back pained tears.

The being before him opened a concealed palm to reveal the Ouija planchet and spoke in a deep, disembodied voice through Olivia's mouth. "I am god."

Then without another second to pass, Jason's neck was violently twisted until an ear-splitting snapping sound was heard. Olivia then relaxed her body and she floated slowly back to the ground while Jason's body hit the floor loudly causing the unlit candles to fall over. Olivia looked behind her and without a single motion caused the candles to all ignite simultaneously causing a corner of Olivia's floor rug to catch a blaze. As the room behind her began to go up in smoke, she floated down the stairs and out of the house.

As she exited the house, a neighborhood boy ran up to her and exclaimed with glee, "Happy Halloween Olivia!"

Without a word, she looked at the young boy before turning her attention back towards the house as the glow of fire began to spread throughout the house. As more and more people began to notice the growing flames and billowing smoke coming from the Morris household, Olivia twisted back towards the boy. Wordlessly, she lifted a single finger to her lips and walked away with the crackling embers of the house illuminating the night sky.

THE END

CASE SIX

IT LURKS IN THE PICTURES

DALE OCAMPO'S FACE glowed in the light of his multiple computer monitor set - up contrasting with the darkness of the room around him. He lets out a harsh yawn and brushes his curly brown hair from his eyes. He leans away for a moment to crack the bones in his hands and in his back hoping to relieve some of the pressure that had been building up from a lack of movement. He'd been up since the dark hours of the morning and unbeknownst to him, the sun was now at its zenith outside of his New York apartment.

He took a moment's reprieve from his work to take a glance around his apartment. He'd only moved in two days ago but had made less progress than he was happy with in terms of his unpacking. Boxes and bags were strewn about half open and spilling out clothes that he had rifled through and dishes he had used for his takeaway.

He exhaled through his nose and said aloud to himself "We really need to get this mess organized." He swiveled in his chair back to facing his monitors, "Right after we get done with you." He said again to himself as he began clicking away on his keyboard and moving his cursor with his mouse. Currently, he was editing a music video for local band.

The music was cringe inducing to him, but he was glad to have found work so quickly after arriving. Freelance photography and video editing were not a viable career in his hometown, so he resolved to make his trek to the Big Apple. With it came a sense of security and validation that his true passion could really be his career, especially now that he was getting paid to do more than photograph distant relatives' weddings and children's birthday parties.

His parents always had their apprehensions about his decision to pursue this lifestyle, particularly his father. Dale always had a feeling that he was something of a disappointment to him. His father was something of a local legend with multitudes of sporting achievements and thousands of fishing stories that always made him a social paragon. Everyone in his home knew the O'Campo name, which is the only reason that Dale was ever recognized for anything. Born naturally timid and anxious, he preferred to spend most of his young life in the company of few friends while sitting in front of his television or his computer. When he announced at the tender age of fifteen that he wanted to pursue a career in photography and filmmaking, he received a verbal assault by his father about what a foolish decision he was making and that he'd be stuck living in their basement forever.

The words stung for a long time and Dale resented him for it, but he found compassion in his sister, Vary. She had always encouraged him to press on and was the one who finally convinced him to leave home to make a name for himself. For that, he was forever in her debt.

Suddenly, from the corner of his monitor he notices a chat notification. He pulls it open and sees that it is none other than Vary reaching out.

"How are you liking New York?" the message said plainly.

"I'm really liking it! I'm actually working on a project right now." Dale wrote back enthusiastically.

"Oh yeah? That's great! What is it?"

"I'm editing a music video for some local death metal band. They're kind of terrible, but money is money." He chuckled to himself, reading aloud as he wrote.

"Awesome! Be sure to send it to me when it's done so I can give mom and dad a heart attack ha ha."
Dale tightened up for a moment, thinking about what his parents must be saying to everyone about him now.

"Will do, and let them know I'm doing okay, yeah? Just this project alone will cover my shopping for two weeks and I've got a few more propositions I'm waiting to hear back about that will cover everything else. They don't need to worry about wiring me money or anything."

"Dale, it's fine. They're not worried about your finances. I told them you're going to do great things over there."

He swallowed back the lump in his throat, "Thanks, V. I've got to get back at it, but maybe you can call me later tonight?"

"Sure thing, talk soon!"

And just like that, the green circle by her name went grey indicating that she was no longer online. A rumbling in his stomach told him however that work could wait, and now it was time to eat.

He made his way into the kitchen and opened the fridge door. In place of food, there was only a few bottles of water, half empty condiment containers, and some nearly rotten vegetables he promised himself he would get to before they went bad. He sighed and opened the freezer above him and pulled a frozen microwave meal from within. The fourth one in two days. He pierced the plastic film with a knife and started heating it. It would take a few minutes, so suddenly stricken with inspiration, he went to the spare room containing the bulk of his packed belongings and brought the boxes out into the living room so that he could start sorting through them.

However, he realized that with the living room already overrun with boxes, he decided that he could store the remaining boxes in the loft above him. The latch to the loft opened effortlessly and he began to place them one by one. He was told about the loft when he first arrived, but never took the time to look around it. He heard the microwave go off, but decided that it needed to cool down anyway, so he might as well have a look around.

Curiously on a small table tucked out of sight, he finds an old school polaroid camera. "I guess the previous tenants left it?" He whispered to himself as he walked over to examine it. As he picked it up, he inspected it but found nothing out of the ordinary. To the contrary, it was in immaculate shape, Dale thought to himself that he could probably use it to market vintage photo shoot and when done, could sell it off for decent pay. Then he looked down, and underneath where the camera was sitting were several dust-coated pictures.

The pictures were of several scenic moments with different families, though it was hard to tell exactly of whom, as the pictures themselves were not nearly as well kept as the camera and had scratches all over them. Dale paid them little mind, thinking that they simply must have been property of whoever owned the camera before moving out. However, amidst the pictures was also a hand-written note.

Dale gently placed the camera back down and picked up the note. In scratchy, frantic handwriting it read "The Camera sees all, even that which is hidden."

Dale scoffed and crumbled the note up before he tossed it back down. He picked up the camera once again and turned to leave. As he made his way back down to collect his dinner, he found himself thinking about the note as he continued inspecting the camera. What could it have possibly meant? Maybe it was just some kind of game made up to scare the kids who used to live here. However, just as he made his way to the kitchen, he heard his phone start vibrating violently at his desk. He walked over and placed the camera down next to his computer, as he lifted the phone, he saw that it was an unfamiliar number.

He thought about just letting it go to voicemail but decided that it might have been a client and it would be in his interest to just answer. He swallowed his phone anxiety down and answered.

"Hello?"

"Hello, is this Dale O'Campo?"

"Yes, it is, how can i help you?"

"This is Amanda Lorentz, I'm with the International Oceanic Exploration and Research Centre. I'm calling you to follow up on your recent application to join our crew aboard our newest research vessel, the *Endurance* to film for a documentary we're putting together. Is that something you're still interested in?"

"Yes, of course! Sorry, I've been busy, but I've been meaning to reach back out to you." Dale was now pacing around his apartment, feeling somewhat anxious as he always does while speaking on the phone.

"No problem at all. Are you still interested in the position? We've had the chance to look at your portfolio and compared to the other applicants, we feel you would be best suited for this position. Most other candidates have either declined or changed their mind, and out of the bunch, yours was the most well put together. So, on behalf of the IOERC, I'd like to offer you the job."

"Yes! That's fantastic!" Dale responded enthusiastically.

"Great! We will get your pre-paid flight tickets and boarding pass sent to you in the coming days, I'll have an email sent out to you with some forms for you to go over and sign. We look forward to having you join us! Take care! Feel free to call us back if you have any questions."

"Will do. Talk to you soon." He replied before hanging up. Finally, Dale went to the kitchen and retrieved his lukewarm food from the microwave. It didn't bother him though, since he was now brimming with excitement and his head danced with fantasies of what accolades he'd receive for the masterpiece he was sure to create. He fluttered back to his computer chair and placed the food down opposite the camera.

He looked at it curiously while chewing a small bite. Then he turned to the computer and began searching for how he could extract the pictures from it. After the better half of an hour, he had it figured out and uploaded the camera's photos to his computer. Excited, he finished off his dinner in a few large bites and began scrolling through the pictures on the screen in front of him.

Dale deduces that the photos have little in common save for the fact that they were taken by the same camera. Curiously though, they date back several years and have been in the hands of several different people and families. As he gets to the last half of the pictures, he stops for a moment to notice that one was dated at only a month ago. The pictures up to that point had been chronological so he wondered what else could be on the camera.

He rationalized that it must have just been more from the previous owner, but as he moved on to the next picture he was greeted with a grisly sight. It was a picture depicting the first family on the photo reel, only in this one the family of four were laying on the ground with their bodies horribly mangled and torn limb from limb. Dale instantly felt nauseous. He wondered for a second if this was some elaborate prank, or a prop from a horror film. Morbid curiosity gripped him, and he scrolled on.

However, indulging his wonder brought him now peace. One by one, each picture showed that of the previous owners all dead in some horrible fashion. One was of a couple hanging by their feet from a window railing with their stomachs cut open and guts spilling out. Another was a picture from high up above where someone had fallen from a tall building becoming a bloody splatter on cement. Another still showed a single person in a bathtub overflowing with blood and water with her throat brutally torn open. The second to last picture

95

was of the last family from a month ago, where their bodies were placed next to each other with their eyes bloodied and faced contorted in a mask of fear and shock.

While all the photos had been chilling, the last one made his hair stand on end and his blood run cold. It was a photo of him. It was as if the camera automatically took his picture when he first entered the loft, because it showed him with his arms full putting down some boxes with his side profile towards where the camera had been sitting.

With his hands shaking, he closes the viewer and turns to look at the camera. "Who took those pictures?" Dale stammered out to himself. He then looks around the room and something connects in his head. All those horrible photos were taken in that apartment. The markings on the walls were identical right down the nicks in the door frames; there was no mistaking it.

Dale was instantly stricken with abject fright. He looked around the once comfortable room but only saw a museum of death. He began nervously searching the web for any articles about mysterious deaths from his apartment complex. Sure enough, after a few changes to his search, he found several articles from obituaries to cold case murder investigations detailing the gruesome ordeals.

Now thoroughly frightened, Dale attempted to call the police hoping that they'd be able to get to the bottom of what was happening. However, as he lifted his phone, he saw that its battery was completely dead, even though he was sure it had an almost full charge only a few minutes ago.

He then quickly dashes to the opposite end of the apartment near the front door to where the apartment's landline was situated and picks it up only to be met with a dead dial tone. Suddenly, he started hearing a strange low hissing noise coming from above him in the loft.

Then following the sound, the power goes out around him, leaving him in darkness. He looks outside but where sun once pierced through the window, now there was only a swirling, inky blackness.

The noises now becoming louder as if moving all around him. In a panic, he remembered the words he read on the note "The Camera sees all, even that which is hidden" and he made a dash to grab the camera. He pointed it to where he heard the sound originating from in the kitchen and snapped a picture. The photo instantly appeared on the camera's screen capturing a strange figure holding the knife he left out on the counter earlier.

Dale quickly dived behind his couch with his back to the thing in the kitchen as the hissing noise began moving around again.
The power in the apartment now begins to flicker furiously, as if the beast was now made aware of him. Slowly he peered out from around the couch and looked into the kitchen but saw nothing other than floating kitchen appliances and all the cutlery from the cutlery drawer, floating in a steady circular fashion.

He raised the camera once again and snapped another picture of where the sound was now coming from. He took another picture and as the picture presented itself, he got a clear image of his stalker. The creature was inhumanly tall but vaguely humanoid. It didn't appear to have any bones, since its figure was impossibly thin, and its skin was nearly translucent. Its face was featureless except for large, gaping hole pulsing with rows of jagged teeth extending and retracting. One hand had seven long fingers that bent with multiple joints and the other arm ended with a long, jagged blade coated in dried blood.

Dale tried to wrap his head around the impossible being before him and dared to take a second picture of it. Only this time, the creature took notice of him, as Dale saw in the photo that its maw and body were now facing him, and he heard that hurried scuttling as it raced towards him. He desperately scrambled to his feet and began to run away from it but felt a sharp, searing pain pierce through his shoulder. He let out a blood-curdling yell as its other hand turned him around. Now that it was upon him, he could see the creature clearly as its maw opened to impossible proportions; its teeth undulating with thick braids of spit coming off them. The creature let out a terrifying roar as it tossed him forcibly to the ground.

He desperately began crawling his way to the large window still obscured by a thick fog and placed his back to it and looked upon the creature. It slowly leaned down to pick up the camera with its long fingers and it clutched it tightly as it raised it up to face him. Dale's breathing became labored as the blood poured from the gaping wound in his shoulder, then he heard the sound of the camera snapping photos, over and over again. Whatever this demon was, it was clearly responsible for the deaths of all those before him.

His mind raced trying to think of what he could do to save himself, but he would not have the chance as the creature suddenly rushed him again. It skewered him again in the stomach with its jagged blade and lifted him into the air. He began coughing up blood as he struggled to free himself, then suddenly the beast flung him through the window with immense strength. As he broke through the glass he was once again greeted by the sunlight as he plummeted to the earth from his fifth story apartment. In his final moments he thought about Vary, his mom, his dad, and about how they would never know the truth and carry on thinking he had taken his own life. He worried that they would think he was a failure. But the last thing he saw was the creature leaning out from above him preparing to snap one final photo to add to its collection as he collided with the ground and everything went black. His mangled copse lay in the street. Blood beginning to pool underneath his head, slowly but surely becoming a slim river that began to run across the pavement. Multiple people ran over to him and stood there in utter horror as someone pulled out their phone to call an ambulance.

CASE SEVEN

THE SHADOW OF FERRIS PARK

THE HEADLIGHTS of a steel gray land rover cut through the pitch-black darkness as the lone vehicle chugged through the dust and dirt of the gravelly road. Inside its cab, Ethan Summerson fiddles with the radio struggling to find the correct frequency as he sifts through muffled, muddy broadcasts of preachers proclaiming the gospel and old timey country music. Finally, he finds what he was looking for as the local news broadcaster's voice projects through his speaker, seemingly in the middle of a sentence.

"-have still not been spotted. So, if you're out near Ferris, please keep an eye out for two young children: Judith and Jacob Sanderson, both ten years old last spotted a week ago when they were leaving their school. They join the list of dozens to have gone missing from Ferris over the course of the last decade. So please if you have any information as to the whereabouts of the Sanderson children or any of the other missing individuals, please contact the authorities and let them know so that those who've gone missing can be reunited with their families."

Ethan let out a long sigh as he shut the radio back off. He was hoping for some miraculous news that maybe they'd been found already, but he knew better than that. He'd been a private investigator for well over twenty years, and never once had anything so convenient happen. It was never anything so simple or innocent. In his experience, if anyone, especially a child, had been missing for more than forty-eight hours he was usually right to assume the worst. He ran his right hand over baggy eyelids and then through his short black and grey hair. He was usually able to keep his emotional distance from cases he'd undertaken as progress in his line of work demanded a cool head. However, he found it difficult now that he was pursuing his missing niece and nephew.

As his phone began ringing in the passenger seat, he snapped back to reality and picked it up. He usually didn't take calls unless they were important, but seeing his cousin Lisa, Jacob and Judith's mother, on his phone certainly qualified as important.

"Lisa, hey." He answered gruffly.

"Ethan, where are you?" She asked with worry heavy on her tone.

"I'm heading up to the abandoned theme park. I'm going to look around for Judith and Jacob."

"Why would you possibly think they'd be up there? That park's been closed for years, they probably wouldn't even know it exists."

"I got a weird thing delivered to my office this morning. A postcard from the theme park that 'Uncle Ethan, we're having so much fun at the park, we can't wait for you to join us' and it was signed with both of their names. I thought it might have been a prank at first, but I compared the handwriting to some old holiday cards they wrote for me and the handwriting was identical."

"I don't know Ethan... have you told the police?"

"The Ferris police? Those clowns who've let how many dozens of people stay missing for over two decades? No, I'm going on my own. At worst I've wasted my time following a dead lead. But if it's something then I have to go after it, Lisa."

Ethan was met with silence for a moment. "Promise me you'll be safe out there, alright?"

"I will... and Lisa?"

"Yeah?"

"I promise I'll bring them home."

She hung up right after hearing him. He looked quizzically at the phone for a moment but decided to just let it go. He knew how he felt about the kids being missing, but he thought about how hard it must've been for her. Afterall, her husband had been out of the picture since before they were even born.

They were all she had, and now they too are gone. His thoughts raced thinking of the multitudes of horrible things that might have happened and how he'd find the words to break the news to her.

As his heart began racing, his breathing became intense and labored, suddenly he felt a coughing fit come over him as his nerves got the better of him. He hoped it would pass, but as his lungs became tight, he had no choice but to quickly sift through his glove box to find an inhaler. As he pressed down on it and felt relief, he reminded himself to be cautious of his asthma, since that was his last inhaler.

Soon the dirt and gravel road disappeared under his headlights and gave way to crumbled, neglected asphalt. As Ethan closed up on his destination, his headlights illuminated the rusted iron gates and the sign above them which read "Ferris Park" featuring a large anthropomorphic cartoon fox; the mascot of the park affectionately called 'Felix the Fox'. After a moment, he put the vehicle in park and stepped out with the lights and engine still running. He made his way up to the gates and inspected them hoping to find a loose bar or an opening he could squeeze through. With his back to the lights of his land rover, his silhouette grew and soon it towered over him. He admired the park's towering buildings and the sheer scale of it. He imagined what it must have been like before it closed.

His daydreaming was interrupted when he heard a sudden rustling in the wood line to his side. He quickly looked over and saw two human shaped shadows that seemed to be watching him from afar. While fumbling to pull out his phone's flashlight, they seemed to dash away, by the time he could shine the light in their direction, there was nothing there.

"Judith!? Jacob!?" He called out desperately, only to be met with silence. He let out an exasperated sigh and decided to turn his attention back to the gate. The gate was sealed shut and was far too heavy for him to open on his own, but as he scoured the grounds, he discovered a hole in the chain-link fence. He felt a wave of relief wash over him that he wouldn't have to scale any great heights. Though, he did wonder if that hole was there from years of natural decay, or if it was made by two children running away from home to play some silly game at a derelict theme park.

Having found his way in, Ethan returned to his vehicle to retrieve some items before he ventured forward. When he got back, he grabbed his voice recorder which he would use to record notes as he went along, and his revolver from the glove compartment. He hoped he would never have to use it, but he didn't know what might be in the steely frame of the park, so he thought it best to be prepared for the absolute worst scenario.

He wished he had an inhaler to take with him, but as he shuffled through his belongings, he let out a frustrated grunt as he turned off the vehicle's lights and engine. He made sure the gun was loaded and that its safety was on, then he tucked it away in a small holster under his armpit. He pulled his grey trench coat up over his shoulders and adjusted the collar of his black turtleneck. He readjusted his socks and tightened the laces of his black boots. Then he pulled out a pair of black leather gloves from his coat pocket and pulled them over his hands. Conditions at the park were foul, and he didn't want to run the risk of accidentally cutting himself and getting an infection, so he thought it would be better to be safe than sorry.

With his phone's flashlight now on and his voice recorder in his other hand he spoke into it. "This is Ethan Summerson, currently following up on a lead for the missing Sanderson twins: Judith and Jacob. It's about 9pm and I'm approaching the abandoned Ferris Park. I am currently going through a hole in the fence to the western side of the entrance." He cut off there as he entered through the portal, feeling an uneasy, creeping sensation crawl over his back like he was being watched.

He whipped back around and saw several more shadows near the vehicle and as he exclaimed "Hey!" at them and shined his light they all scattered, then he spoke again into the recorder.

"Some weird figures were just standing near my car. I thought I saw something earlier near the gate, but I wasn't sure. Could have just been animals, but they looked sort of humanlike. Might also have just been teenagers trying not to get caught. I'll be keeping an eye out." He didn't want to say it out loud because he thought of how ridiculous it might have sounded, but when he saw the figures, he could have sworn some of them had a red glow around where their eyes would be.

Ethan trudged onwards through the hole in the fence which lead him to around the back of the ticket booth. He was able to finesse his way around overturned debris and half collapsed building all worn out from years of structural neglect. Then he found himself looking headlong into the park as the hundreds of visitors must have done so long ago. Only, where they faced a glowing park teeming with life and merriment, he was now faced with the defunct skeletal remains that howled as the wind echoed through its countless hollow aisles.

As he walked past the empty ticket booth, he grabbed a dusty, moth eaten map off the counter that had been miraculously not totally faded beyond the point of legibility. Most of the whimsical names of rides and attractions were tough to make out, but he was able to surmise that if he simply moved forward he would make it to the heart of the park called "Playland" where everything else would visible to him. He resolved to head that way first to get a solid lay of the land, then he would regroup and formulate his next step. He could not help but notice as he moved upwards that a large, decayed cutout of Felix the Fox stood positioned to greet guests as they'd come his way. In a small compartment on his chest were several small postcards. Ethan picked them all out and inspected them. A chill ran down his spine as he looked them over and realized they were exactly the same as the one he had received from the twins, except these ones were addressed to dozens of different people, each signed off with the names of those who'd been declared missing.

Ethan stopped and shined his light all around him as the feeling of being watched crept over him. He was thoroughly disturbed by his findings and deep down was glad he'd thought to bring his firearm.

"Just found something big." He stated into the recorder. "There's big goofy cutout of the park's mascot near the entrance and it had a bunch of postcards like the one I got. Each one was signed by people who I can only assume went missing around Ferris. I don't know what exactly that implicates, but it's definitely not normal." He paused and looked around for a moment before going continuing. "I'm starting to get pretty creeped out around here. Feels like I'm being constantly watched but I don't hear or see anything. Going to keep moving on. Hope I find the kids fast."

Finally, Ethan found himself in the central area; the Playland. From his position he was able to look around in a perfect circular motion and make out the silhouettes of various defunct attractions. Something called the "Water Rush", which was a waterlog ride. The flying swings called the "Fantasy Flight" most of which had fallen off their cables and simply rested on the ground where they had fallen; the overgrown vines indicated that they had been there for years. Of course, there was the titular Ferris Wheel, the namesake and iconic scenic ride which towered over the entire park. It was the first thing he saw as he had driven up to the park. Finally, there was a large structure near the rear of the park which displayed several torn-up fabric signs and several small, rusted merchandise and concession stands.

Ethan was in awe of the park and felt at a loss for a moment as he speculated about where to investigate first. However, not wanting to waste time, he resolved to pick a direction and just go. "I'm heading into the east side of the park near the broken-down water ride. I'm going to make long sweeps through and hopefully find something." He spoke into the recorder once again. He felt a sense of comfort in the voice recordings. It was almost like having somewhere there with him. Then suddenly a sound rang out from several yards away. It was a child's scream followed by disembodied, hurried footsteps. Ethan's heart raced as he picked up his pace hoping to identify the source as the sound but just as quickly as it came, so too did silence take its place.

As Ethan rushed around calling out to the mysterious voice and as he checked around every corner, he found nothing. With his pace slowing down, he took a momentary break to catch his breath as he looked around and listened carefully. Then, he heard something new. Low, unintelligible chanting. Rhythmic and eerie as the many voices went on, he was deeply disturbed and even drew his firearm fearing that he might run into a dangerous group. He cautiously moved around corners keeping his light low so as not to draw any unwanted attention.

"There's some weird shit going on here. I just heard a kid yelling out and running around; I couldn't find them but now there's some kind of fuckin' cult or something out here chanting! I can't tell what they're saying." He let out a sudden anguished grunt as he finished his sentence. He lifted his hand up to his face and felt a cold wet spot under his nose. He lifted his phone's light up and sure enough his nose had suddenly begun to bleed profusely.

He stared in surprise for a moment before he felt his vision going in and out. At first, he thought it was his phone's light going faulty, but as his conscious thoughts became spacey and before he knew it, he collapsed to the ground struggling to maintain consciousness as the chanting of voices became louder and louder until they were deafening. He felt his grip slipping as his firearm, voice recorder and phone fell to the ground. He shut his eyes tightly, then all noise around him stopped and he opened his eyes once again.

As his eyes reopened, they could barely conceive what they were taking in. The park he was in had changed drastically. The black night sky had been replaced a stark white with shifting, inky black clouds like a Rorschach test. The park itself seemed to be inexplicably repaired to its original state with moving rides and fresh coats of paint, though strangely there was no sound, like a silent film. The scene baffled Ethan's mind as he meekly looked around then he saw two sets of eyes peeking out from behind a colorful stand. As they notice that he's spotted them, they dip away out of sight. But he was sure of it, they were Judith and Jacob.

"Judith!? Jacob!? It's me! It's Uncle Ethan!" He exclaimed with his cool, professional shell now completely gone as he quickly went over. As he approached however, no one was there. But as he whipped around, he saw them again as they dodged and dipped away. He continued to give chase calling out to them as he did. Then finally after he thought he'd cornered them successfully; they had escaped him yet again as he saw them running away into the glowing maw of a scary clown with long fangs with a sign above it reading the "The Horror House". Then as they disappeared into the darkness, he heard the voice of Judith call out,

"Come and find us!"

He took another step before the fainting sensation from before as his senses faded out and in like the tides of an ocean. He struggled to maintain consciousness, but after a momentary blink, he was back to where he was before he awoke. Slumped over with his head pounding and his shirt stained from the steady drip of his nosebleed. He looked up in a daze and felt a new sensation as the misty droplets of rain landed gently on his face as distant thunder rolled over the sky. Slowly he brought himself to his feet, gathered his things, and looked around to gather his bearings.

A figure stood opposite Ethan. While his faculties were not all together yet, he definitely knew that silhouette was not there before he passed out. He studied it carefully, then raised his phone's light up to it to get a better view. The light revealed a figure wearing a costume of Felix the Fox. Its red fur was frayed and stained with dried blood, more apparent against the dirty white stomach area. Its cartoonish eyes glowed an ominous dull red and its plastic smiling tooth were crooked, broken, and sharp.

Ethan stared at the figure, wondering if it was real or merely a hallucination. Then the figure's head tilted to the side curiously as Ethan began to move away. Stricken with shock, Ethan tripped to the ground then began scrambling back to his feet. With his eyes fixed on Felix, he saw as Felix raised one of its furry paws and wag a single finger as it shook its head side to side. Then with the other hand, it produced a heavy, bloodstained axe. Suddenly it erupted into a manic, cackling laughter as it dashed away behind the rides into the darkness.

Stricken with panic and confusion, Ethan looked around with his back pressed up against a wall.

He had little time to collect himself though as he suddenly heard a barrage of hurried footsteps before another figure burst from around the corner and came at him. A hooded figure wearing a decayed plastic Felix mask grabbed Ethan by the neck and began thrashing him around. Ethan resisted as best he could despite his fear but found himself outmatched as the masked figure bashed his head against the control panel of a nearby ride. As the figure rushed at him again, Ethan was able to recover just long enough to turn around and throw a heavy fist at the head of the masked figure, cracking the mask and sending the assailant to the ground and himself with him. He stood up quickly and reached into his holster to draw his gun. But before he can bring the gun into aim, he feels the burning sensation as a blade slashes across his arm as he accidentally pulls the trigger firing off into the distance.

He recoils and looks up to see a second attacker brandishing a large knife dripping with his blood. The attacker then rushes him and goes for the gun, pushing Ethan against an adjacent wall. Ethan feels his grip slipping with the searing pain radiating from his cut, but in a burst of strength, he was able to bring the gun forward and fires a round directly under the chin of the bladed attacker. The initial assailant notices that Ethan now had the gun aimed at the ready and begins to run away but is unable to escape as Ethan fires three rounds, missing the first two while the third hit the assailant in the leg.

The masked attacker recoils in pain but does not produce a sound as it quickly dashed back around the corner that it initially came from. With a moment's reprieve, Ethan took the opportunity to demask and identify the attacker who laid dead before him. Ethan's mind retreated as he looked upon the bloodied face of a young man whose face he recognized as one of the missing children from several years ago.

He steps back while putting a hand to his head as he struggled to comprehend what he was witnessing. As he shook his head, the park jumped to life.

Suddenly all the music played simultaneously and horribly out of tune through staticky muffled speakers. The lights flashed on and off through dull and dusty orange and red lightbulbs. Then as Ethan looked around his blood ran cold as he noticed dozens upon dozens of hooded figures surrounding him, all wearing the smiling face of Felix with glowing red LED lights affixed around their eyes.

"What the fuck do you want!?" Ethan screamed with terror in his voice.

They gave no answer, they merely stared silently, waiting for his next move. In a desperate move, Ethan raised the gun up and steadied himself as he panned side to side locking onto one masked figure then the next. Eventually, they began moving towards him, slowly and silently one step after another. In a sudden outburst, Ethan fired a round into the crowd but does not hit the target. He backs up a bit as he notices their pace quickening. He went to pull the trigger again but heard only the heart-wrenching sound of the hammer clicking against nothing. He was out of ammunition.

Suddenly the figures began to give chase. Ethan quickly whipped around and began to run away as he dashed and dodged through various stands and structures in an attempt to outrun his pursuers.

Then a familiar old enemy made itself known. As the chase went on, Ethan felt his chest tightening up as he struggled to catch his breath.

"Shit! Not now!" Ethan whispered to himself as he struggled to keep his pace. His asthma was seriously affecting him, and he knew he would not be able to run for much longer, let alone fight once they caught up. As if calling out to him, a light appeared from the distance. The light came from The Horror House, just as it had from his dream.

The oscillating lights out of synch with its muddied, eerie carnival music called out to him offering a boon. He felt that his dream was a vision of what he needed to do. So, he laid low waiting for his moment to move. He stayed perfectly still waiting for several pairs of footsteps to pass him by. After a while, the silence had convinced him that it was his time to go, so he made a break for the haunted house attraction hoping that it would be his salvation from this nightmare.

As Ethan approached, the scene gave him no respite. The masked figures were there all waiting for him. Just as still as they had been earlier, they were now lined up double file on either side of the entrance with their glowing eyes all fixed on him. He saw the one with the bloodied leg nearest to him slightly hunched over, clearly unable to put its whole weight on its leg. Ethan knew there was no running. His destiny was calling, and whether or not he liked it, he had to answer. So, after a long hesitation he made his way forward keeping his eyes fixed on the masked figures. He stopped just a few yards from them before trying his luck.

"Are they in there? Judith and Jacob?" He asked somberly, dreading what their answer might be.

"They are with Felix. They have been waiting for you." They spoke one word at a time between the various figures like a broken choir. He examined the exterior of the building. It was three floors tall with corny Halloween decorations displayed in various poses. The childlike nature of the building juxtaposed with the dreadful sensation the masked figures gave off made Ethan's hair stand on end.

"What am I going to find in there?" He asked anxiously.

"Felix will find you. Just like he found us. We are his children. And so are you."

Ethan swallowed the lump in his throat and pressed onwards past the masked figures up to the howling entrance bellowing out the disfigured carnival sounds fixed with ambient Halloween sounds like doors creaking and witches cackling. He hesitated for a moment before going in. He thought about just turning around and making a mad dash back to the car. He thought he might be able to call the police and be done with this. But deep down he knew that was not an option. If he turned around and somehow made it out with his life, he would live forever with the guilt of knowing he ran away and left his niece and nephew to suffer whatever fate befell them at the hands of a gang of masked cultists. He resolved that he'd rather die than live a life like that, so he entered the darkness of The Horror House.

As he became engulfed in the darkness, the two masked figures near the entrance slowly closed the door behind him, and as they did all light and sound disappeared, leaving him all alone in the silent darkness. His flashlight cut through the darkness illuminating derailed and rusted carts that once creeped along their tracks. Some animatronics permanently left out where they once would pop out to startle the riders. But as Ethan moved his way through, the most disturbing thing to him, was the stench of rot, decay, and death that lingered heavy on the air. He pushed a large jangling skeleton aside as he made his way deeper down the labyrinthine corridors struggling to keep his directions clear as he went.

Outside he heard the wind and rain crashing against the thin, rotten frame of the attraction as thunder crackled over head in a low, booming roar. Then another sound caught his attention. The screams of children cut through the atmospheric silence like a knife. Instantly Ethan knew it was from Judith and Jacob. In a panicked rush, Ethan flew up the stairs through the emergency access stairway all the way to the top floor where the frantic voices of the two children called out to him by name.

As he burst through the doorway the voices suddenly stopped. Fearing the worst, he called back out to them, but was met with silence. He hurriedly rushed through the floor sweeping every room looking for any sign of them. Finally, he came up to the last room he had not checked and with an immense feat of strength, he kicked open the door and surveyed the scene. The room was littered with debris and he could hear the muffled whimpering of children. He quickly dashed into the room and found them both curled up under the desk. He found himself unable to speak, equal parts relieved to have found them alive, and horrified to see their scared bruised forms curled up with eyes all puffed up and bloodshot from crying and screaming.

"Oh god... oh god... I'm so glad you're okay! It's alright, everything's alright. Uncle Ethan is here, guys. I'm not going to let anything happen to you." Ethan mumbled as he reached his arms out to embrace them.

"Uncle Ethan!" Judith exclaimed as her eyes darted behind Ethan before she clenched up with Jacob in her arms.

Without sound or warning, the figure in the bloody Felix suit descended upon Ethan punching him to the ground with immense force. Ethen reached out to get hold of the ground so that he could lift himself back up, but then felt the sharp crushing stop of the mascot's foot as it dug its heel into his hand, shattering the bones with a loud, blood-curdling crack.

He lets out a loud, anguished yell before he is able to free himself and roll over to his other side. But before he could climb to his feet again, he felt a heavy, cutting blow made to his thigh. The pain he felt was unlike any other he'd ever felt in his life. He was unable to scream; he could merely open his mouth in soundless anguish as he examined the axe that had been buried into his leg.

The mascot let go its handle and put its hands up to its jagged mouth pantomiming that it was stifling its hysterical laughter like a twisted cartoon. In an act of desperation, Ethan pulled the axe from his leg while the mascot recoiled in its laughing fit. With one mighty swipe, Ethan lunged forward and dug the blade of the axe directly into its neck, feeling pulpy, squelching, wet matter as he did so.

He watched as a river of blood poured from its neck making loud plopping noises as heavy droplets of blood pooled at its feet. From outside, over the crackling thunder he heard the anguished, angry screaming and chanting of the cultists as they began banging on the front door.

He dragged his way over to the children to check on them and as he did, he began smelling the unmistakable scent of smoke then saw the snaking black vapors from outside the opposite window. He surmised that somehow the cultists knew their god had been injured and now they wanted revenge and planned to make the haunted house their graves. Ethan had little time to get the children onto their feet before he once again felt the crushing blast of force as a bloody paw grabbed hold of his head and smashed it through the nearest window. Before his sense could come back, the beast pulled him back in and lifted him up off his feet before spinning and throwing him through the doorway into the hall.

"Uncle Ethan!" the kids cried hoarsely.

"Get through the window and get out of here!" He replied as the blood from his wounds poured down his face.

Ethan is able to scoot back and pull his back to the wall as Felix approached him, still gushing blood from its neck wound. With the menacing figure standing over him with the axe raised skyward about to finish the job, he didn't notice as Jacob had slinked into the room behind them.

"Felix?" Jacob asked meekly.

The mascot's head swiveled all the way around before its body turned to face the boy. It looked down at him quizzically as it took notice of the small Felix the Fox plush doll he had presented to it. Then in a surprising act, Felix dropped its weapon and knelt down to examine the doll as Jacob shyly handed it over. Ethan saw their one final chance at escape and went for it. He lurched forward and grabbed hold of the axe's handle and swiped at Felix's back digging the axe deep into its spine. He heard it recoil in pain as it scrambled to regain its footing, but Ethan was already upon it. Again, and again he hacked and mangled the mascot suit as geysers of blood exploded forth painting him and Jacob in sheets of red ichor. He took no notice of the horror on the boy's face watching as he continued his onslaught. Finally convinced that the deed was done, and with smoke now crawling its way up into the third floor Ethan called out to the children.

"Get out of here! Go through the window and run as far away as you can!" He screamed as he collapsed to the floor, weary from his wounds.

He didn't hear any response, but he managed to see their feet moving quickly and he was hopeful that they had made their escape. Then he was alone with the bloodied, mangled remains of Felix the Fox. His vision began to fade and his consciousness with it. But before he could rest, the glowing red LED eyes snapped back to life once again. He used every last burst of strength to pull himself away and right himself back upright using a nearby table to support his weight.

He watched as the chopped up remains pulled themselves back up and twisted itself back into position facing him. It began to let out a gurgling laughter as it fixated upon him. Then for his final act, Ethan lunged himself forward and speared himself and Felix out of the opposite window and sent both careening towards the ground. Hitting it with a loud, painful thud. Knocking him uncounouss. For an un-specified amount of time, Ethan was Out cold. But the fire was still at it's prime. He woke up some time later after the plunge and felt his body as pain covered it's entirety, as though it had given up.

There was no more resistance to be had. Whatever happened next would be it for him. There were no more tricks up his sleeve. He watched as The Horror House glowed with orange and red flames as they climbed towards the sky in sheets of thick, glowing smoke.

He turned over one last time to face his opponent. His heart sunk as dread became the only thing present. Sharply its eyes came back to life with a dull red glow as the shredded pieces of the suit slowly began pulling themselves away to reveal the ravaged body of a person inside it. The stained, filthy fur began to climb over Ethan's body. He tried to protest, but he had no strength. As the head piece enveloped him, he felt his breathing stop, but his mind continued to race. He saw every abominable act perpetrated by the demonic suit. The mental anguish was more than Ethan could bear. He wanted the pain to stop and to put the nightmare to rest, but then, on splintered bones he felt the suit lifting itself up with him inside it. It looked down and revealed the twisted face of the previous occupant permanently locked in an expression of abject horror, the body rotten and disfigured.

He realized this was his fate. He screamed wildly but could not stop. With one foot after the other, the suit began to pick up pace as it made its way over to the red and blue flashing lights where police were arriving on scene.

He approaches the two officers and begins to call out begging for help. But all they can hear is the menacing laughter of the suit as it drew near the unsuspecting officers.

"Stop Right there and put your hands up!" demanded the female officer as she un-holstered her service weapon and aimed it at the suit. When the officer was within range the suit rushed with inhuman speed towards her. Ethan felt unfathomable agony as his bones twisted and broke with each of its movements. He begged for help, but the laughter only grew louder. The suit swooped down on her and lifted her up with both hands. Ethan felt his hands being used to strangle the woman before the bones in her neck cracked and twisted under his grasp.

He screamed in agony as the other officer fumbled to pull out his gun and fired several shots at Ethan in the suit. He felt each of the bullets piercing through him and he prayed that the burning sensation as they tore through his flesh would be enough to put him out of his misery, but it proved unsuccessful in stopping the suits advance. With the first officer dispatched, it deftly made its way over to the other, unphased by the hail of gunfire.

"No! No! Stop!" Ethan begged as the suit took hold of the officer's head and started slamming it viciously in the door of his patrol cruiser. Repeatedly until only bloody, chunky remains of brain and skull matter remained.

Ethan could not stop himself from weeping profusely pleading that something could stop him. Then from the shadows several figures approached wearing Felix masks. The cultists returned and offered two gifts to their master. Held firm in their grasp were the panicked shaking bodies of Judith and Jacob.

"No! No! No! God, no!" Ethan screamed until his lungs gave out and he could only cough up blood.

His vision began to fade as his eyes became glued shut from his tears. The last thing he was able to make out was the suit extending its bloodied hand out to the children, as their small hands slowly and anxiously stretched out, **GRIPPING HIS**...

CASE EIGHT

THE MORNING SUN crept through the blinds and painted Caleb and Amy Rafferty in soft stripes of light. Caleb, always the early riser, rustled slowly from his slumber until his eyes cracked open. As they adjusted to the low light, he read the time on the clock; it was only a few minutes past six. He felt a rush of blood and excitement go through him. Today was the day.

In only twenty-four short hours he would be on the smooth asphalt competing in the Sebastian Alonzo Memorial Race. Quickly and quietly, he pulled himself from the bed and began his morning routines. In the bathroom he brushed his teeth for two minutes; no more, no less. He took his razor and trimming sheers and sculpted his bedraggled beard into the short, well-kempt form that Amy was fond of.

Following a brief, cold shower, he positioned his short brown hair into its usual style, taking a moment of thought as he stares into the bathroom mirror and Exhales deeply before exiting.

Then as he made his way into the kitchen, he was met with the intoxicating scent of eggs, bacon, and hashed potatoes. He hastily seated himself at the table and watched as Amy worked her magic.

"So, what's on the menu this morning?"

"Only the best for today's soon-to-be first place driver." She said with a smile as her tired eyes focused intensely on the food in front of her.

"First place? Oh, I was thinking I'd just take fourth and call it a day." He sarcastically replied with a chuckle.

"Well I'm not staying married to fourth place. Guess I'll just pack all this up and give it to whoever wins, and I'll just go home with them."

"In that case, I suppose I'll just have to win. Racing is easy, cooking on the other hand? Now that's tough."

"That's why we're a good team." She said as she gently placed a plate full of food in front of him.

"Thank you." He said excitedly with a forkful of eggs already close to his mouth.

Amy made her own plate and took her seat at the table right beside him and turned on the television. As Caleb shoveled away his breakfast his eyes danced around their house examining all the pieces of racing memorabilia they had collected throughout the length of their relationship. Along every wall were pictures of iconic racers and their cars, schematics of engines, and framed photos of historic racing events. But one catches his attention more than the others.

Positioned directly below their wall mounted television was an unassuming photo of Caleb posing with his junior racing team the Track Wolves. He glanced over his youthful face brimming with joy. At the time he was barely old enough to drive, but ever since he was a child, he thought of nothing other than racing. All of his family were diehard fans, but his eldest brother, Luke, truly sparked his interest in making a career out of it.

He raced in a casual league and sometimes took Caleb out for practice runs. It was there, with the screeching of tires and stench of burnt rubber that his passions blossomed into obsession. The day he was old enough to join the Track Wolves he called and called every day until they relented and let him try out. To his dismay and embarrassment, the first two times he tried out he failed miserably. Perhaps due to nerves or simply inexperience behind the wheel.

But on the third time, he had something to show for. While some of the more senior members of the team had their reservations, their hesitations melted away the day that he took home the gold at the regional competition. That was the day immortalized on their mantle.

"Honey, look!" Amy exclaimed as she excited slapped his bicep.

Caleb snapped out of his daydreaming to look up at the television screen. He saw the slender face of Sebastian Alonzo as he spoke to a reporter through the grainy lens of a camera from decades ago. Caleb recognized the scene instantly. It was an interview from Sebastian's first major win on the circuit. At the time, he was still considered an up and comer, and many at the time thought he was arrogant. However, seventeen championships and twenty-nine years later, he would become known as one of the greatest drivers of all time.

"Sebastian, a lot of people are saying that you're a flash in the pan, what do you have to say to them?" The reporter asked through the cacophonous cheers of a surrounding crowd.

"I'd say, it's hard to hear them from all the way behind me."

Caleb smirked when Alonzo said that line. He'd watched that interview dozens of times, and each time he could dream of what witty thing he'd say if he was ever in that position. The scene on the television played out with clips of his racing highlights as audio from various interviews played over them.

His eighth-generation car blazed down the track with its brilliant red color and bright orange number 06. Eventually playing out into the grisly moment when his demise was broadcast to thousands. Due to a faulty repair on his car's roll cage, his life came to a sudden tragic ending when a rival racer accidentally caused his car to spiral out of control. Then, the screen went black as the voice of Alonzo played once more taken from another interview.

"When you're in the lead, you don't look back, only forward. That's the way I want to live my life."

Finally, the words rolled out across the screen: The Sebastian Alonzo Memorial Race. Amy looked over and saw Caleb glowing with excitement as he read the words. A slight smile crept over her face as she weaved her arm around his and pulled herself into a gentle embrace.

"I'm so proud of you, Caleb. I always knew you'd get your shot to make it big."

He smiled as he pulled her in tighter. "I couldn't do it if I didn't have you in my corner."

He hesitated for a moment as she conjured the nerve to say what was on her mind. "I don't mean to sound like a downer right before your big day, but I'm a little worried."

"What for?"

"Well, I mean it's dangerous out there. Seeing what happened to Sebastian, knowing it could happen to you, I just get a little nervous."

He brushed her long dark hair from her face and gave her a peck on the forehead. "I know, but I promise I'll be fine. Cars are a lot safer now than they were back when he was racing. If something was wrong with the car the crew would catch it way before it hit the track."

She simply looked up into his eyes and saw them shimmer as he began to talk about the mechanics of the vehicles and gave him a slight grin. However, as he went on and on, suddenly his phone began to ring from the kitchen table. "You worry too much." He said with a grin as he kissed her forehead before rising to answer.

"Hello?"

"Caleb! It's Sam."

"I have caller ID, Sam, I know it's you when you call." He replied with a chuckle.

"Wise ass..." The voice trailed off. The man on the other end was Caleb's mentor and team owner, Samuel Irons, of the titular Irons

Motorworks. "Listen, I know today's the big day and I wanted to check in on ya'."

"Doin' great, Sam. I could not be more excited for the race; I just know this one is going to jump us to the big leagues."
"I'm glad to hear your enthusiasm but pluck and luck ain't enough to win a race. When can you get down to the track, I've got the team all here already with the car, and I want you to get used to it before show time."

"I'm out the door already. Can't wait to see that beauty in person!"

"Good, see ya' soon."

As Caleb ended the call, he looked over excitedly to Amy who was twisted around on the couch listening in on his conversation. "Get dressed and ready babe, we're hitting the track."

It took the pair little time to make it to their destination. What would usually have been a twenty-minute drive was hastily chopped down several minutes by Caleb's excited, if a touch reckless driving. There were very few drivers out that early anyway, but it would have made little difference to Caleb. With the hum of his engine and every mile that ticked on the odometer, he felt he was that much closer to his destiny. And as they pulled up to the towering gates, the unlit signs signified they had arrived.

The Orion Speedway, famous in many ways for the phenomenal races that had taken place on its hallowed grounds. However, for as many sterling achievements as it boasted, there would forever loom a shadow to tarnish its brilliant reputation.

This was the very track where Sebastian Alonzo had lost his life in that tragic accident which had taken place so many years ago. Now, as far as Caleb was concerned, it was going to be remembered for something new; it would be known as the proving grounds where the next greatest racer would earn his title.

The sun was now fully shining as it reached its height above the horizon. Caleb had parted from Amy and made his way down to the track while she took a seat in the empty bleachers where she'd have the perfect view. Caleb hurried his steps as he saw familiar faces crowded around a large, covered object.

"You're late!" Sam exclaimed as he reached out an open hand to shake Caleb's. "How you feelin' today, son? Anxious at all?"

"Not at all, I've got nerves of steel! My hands are shakin' from excitement, though." He replied with a chuckle.

"Well come on over here and let's take a look at what's behind door number one."
And with a confirmatory nod from Sam, the crew carefully removed the heavy black tarp from the object. What was underneath left Caleb's jaw hanging as he looked over it. He studied its smooth curvature over the long, sturdy frame; it was a mustang, one of Caleb's personal favorites.

He took in its stunning black matte paint accentuated with brilliant, thick red stripes going down its length. Various sponsor decals read out several notable names including *SolarDarkFilms* and *Kalen Industries*. The pièce de resistance was the number written on either side of the car; in striking orange and gold colors was the only number Caleb had ever cared about: 01.

He stood there for a while in stunned silence before he finally spoke. "This might singlehandedly be the most gorgeous piece of machinery I've ever seen."

Sam had a hearty gut laugh as he reached over to pat the young man on his back. "I had a feeling' you'd like it. Now, this here is a ninth gen build, so it's going to run a bit different than what you're used to. Part of the reason I called you out here so early was so you could get behind the wheel and give her a test run. You're already familiar with the gentlemen with me: Pete, Mark, Stewart, and Matt. These boys are going to be our lifeline today, they'll take good care of ya'."

Caleb went through one by one, making some small talk with each of them. He'd met them before but had not worked directly with them.

He'd seen them on the track for other racers on the team and knew each of them were more than competent. Having seen the car and the team, any doubts Caleb held had melted away and left him feeling refreshed with renewed vigor and a redoubled sense of confidence. He was not just going to win; he was going to make a name for himself.

It took him no time to climb into the driver's seat and wrap his fingers around the steering wheel. As he looked at the various dials and levers, Sam leaned into the window.

"Now, Caleb. Remember when you're out there, the world is watching. Think of this as a qualifying run. Do the best you can, and you'll climb to a higher starting position. Now, get out there and show us what you're capable of."

And as he leaned away from the vehicle, he ushered the team with him and gave Caleb the thumbs up. Caleb scanned the empty stands and saw his wife staring expectantly, and with a smile he turned the ignition and heard the roar of the engine as the beast came to life. He slowly set the car into motion and made his way to the starting line. He was given a countdown, then he was off. He blazed down the asphalt like a bat out of hell. The car flew so smoothly that it felt weightless. Caleb could hardly contain himself as the wheels glided across the ground in an elegant dancer on a stage.

"Caleb! It's Matt. We're all going to be on the two-way, so we can give you feedback and advice as the race goes on."

"Awesome! This thing is amazing, y'all are going to have to pry me out of here if you ever want it back!"

"Stew here, we're all glad to hear you're diggin' it. Just be careful alright? She's fast, but she can't really take a beating out there, so try to avoid any and all contact or you'll be out of luck. The tires will last you a full tank, so don't worry about that. And the tank should last you a while, but we'll be monitoring you, so we'll let you know when it's time to come home to roost."

"Thanks guys, the only way we'll lose this is through an act of god."

"Or if your big head weighs the car down." Sam interjected met with the laughter of the crew.

"once I take home the gold, I'll be getting a lot of offers, so I'd watch what I say if I were you."

"Sure thing, champ." He replied sarcastically, "When you're a big star I'll make sure to hang up a signed poster of you at my daughter's unicorn ranch."

Caleb caught himself laughing hard enough at the old timer's wit that the car began to swerve just a bit. As he regained his composure, he caught himself looking up into the stands as he rounded the next corner hoping to see Amy. She was sitting as far forward as she could with her hands covering her ears watching as he blew past her, but the smile on his face as he passed her quickly faded as he saw something else unusual in the stands. He was sure that no one else was there besides him, Amy, and the crew, but for a moment, he thought he saw someone else standing right by the fence separating the stands from the track. As he looked into his rearview mirror, he saw nothing.

"He guys, we're the only ones here right?"

"Should be unless some of the other racers started pulling in. Why?" Pete replied quizzically.

"Yeah, but no one else would be in the stands, right?"

"No one except your wife." Mark rebutted decisively.

"That's weird then... could have sworn I saw someone in racing gear standing back there, but when I looked back, I didn't see anything."

"Guess it's just the ghost of Sebastian Alonzo." Sam cackled into the headset. "Getting spooked out there? Seeing things? If you want, I can probably take your place."

"Hardy-har-har. I thought it was a race, not a night at the Apollo?" Caleb snapped back to the howling of the team. They must have been right though, he rationalized to himself. His mind was probably just playing tricks on him. With each lap he made around the track, Caleb felt more and more comfortable behind the wheel. He understood its intricacies and even had the rest of the crew convinced that he was a natural with the machine.

Having pulled the car back into the garage for maintenance, Sam had insisted that Caleb go home and have dinner and relax for the rest of the afternoon since he would not need to be back at the track until later that evening. He begrudgingly accepted, but not without protesting that he'd rather stay the whole time with the team to help where he could. But to Amy's silent relief he was rebutted.

The few hours at their home, all he could do was anxiously pace around with his eyes glued to the clock, watching as every minute passed by. While he was usually very talkative around the dinner table, Amy noted that he seemed uncharacteristically withdrawn. However, she understood that his mind weighed heavy with anticipation, so she did her best to give him his space. Finally, the hour drew near, and it was time to get ready for the main event. With otherworldly haste, Caleb and Amy made their way back to the Orion Speedway. As they pulled up, they were struck by how drastically different it was from that morning. Now with twilight sun setting the arena's neon lights and LED screens were blinding.

There were hundreds of people everywhere they looked, holding concessionary food and drink, smiling, and laughing with jovial merriment. Picturing the idea that their countless eyes would be fixed on him made him both extraordinarily excited and equal parts nervous. However, there was little time for that, as they made their way to the racers' VIP area.

Caleb admired himself in his lounge's mirror. His racing outfit fit perfectly. The black sleeves were covered in sponsorship logos with its crimson red torso brandishing the team logo featuring a large wolf tearing through steel bars. The legs matched the color scheme, being primarily red with thick black stripes going down his thighs. He always liked the suit, he thought it made him look cool, even though Amy always teased him for its appearance, This time, she just watched him in silent adoration as he pridefully took himself in. This would be the man that was on the front covers of magazines and cereal boxes for years to come. It all depended on this very night.

Suddenly, familiar voices came excitedly ripping through the air as four figures came into the room.

"Caleb!" Screamed the voice of his sister Chloe as she rushed up to him to throw him in a large hug. "C'mon April, come give Uncle

Caleb a hug!" As her young daughter followed shyly putting her arms halfway around his waistline.

"Hi!" Exclaimed Caleb's mother as she greeted Amy with a warm hug before making her way over to Caleb.

Caleb's father slowly entered the room as well, giving Amy a big hug, then extending a hand to shake Caleb's.

"How you doin', big guy?"

"Excited! Maybe a little nervous." Caleb replied with a chuckle.

"Ah, don't be!" his father replied with a firm pap on his shoulder.

"You're going to do great, sweetheart." His mother chimed in softly.

"Ready to head to the track? The guy outside asked us to let you know it was about time before we came in. We just wanted to see you before you went out." Chloe said excitedly.

"Oh shoot, yeah, let's go!" Caleb said as he quickened his pace following the others out the door. As they approached the point where their paths separated, Caleb pulled Amy in for a tight embrace and quick kiss. He gave his mother, sister, and niece all equally heartfelt embraces before his father. His father was not an especially affectionate man, so when he pulled Caleb in for a hug in place of a handshake, he was somewhat taken aback.

"You're gonna make us all proud, son. Go get 'em."

Caleb could only nod as he watched his family making their way to the stands. Once they were out of view, he started making his way to the gate onto the track. As he approached, the roar of the crowd became deafening. All at once, his nerves dissipated and gave way to a cool, calm excitement. He pulled his helmet over his head and briskly jogged out of the fluorescent lights of the tunnel and into the blinding illumination of the towering stadium lights.

Few words were exchanged between Caleb and the rest of the crew; they all knew there was no point to small talk. They were here for the race and that's where all their attentions were focused. Once again, Caleb found himself behind the steering wheel, but this time decked out in his full regalia. With the engine purring steadily, the announcer began to speak.

"Good evening ladies and gentlemen and welcome to the Sebastian Alonzo Memorial Race!" The crowd was now a roaring cacophony of cheers and excited yelling. "This race is dedicated to one of the greatest racers of our time, Sebastian Alonzo. Taken from us all too soon, but even still, in his twenty-nine-year long career he has managed to inspire countless lives. And so, in his memory, thirty-three up-and-coming racers have gathered here today, just as Alonzo himself had before he became a legend. Will one of these young bucks have what it takes to live up to his memory? Tonight, we will find out!"

The words rang in Caleb's head. Then he got the confirmation from Sam to leave the pit lane and start making his way to the track. He watched anxiously as the contending thirty-two racers did the same. He felt a tension unlike any other as the safety car came out with its orange lights flashing in their steady rhythm like a war drum as the combatants met the field. Time felt frozen as the racers made their way around the lap. Three caution laps were customary, but with every passing second, Caleb fought the itch to slam on the accelerator. Finally, they began the third, and final, lap. Sam's voice broke out from the radio in Caleb's helmet.

"Alright, once you get done with this one, you're going to form up double file with the other guys, then once the announcer gives you the go ahead, you floor it. Got it?"

"Yep, then go for the win."

"That's the plan. Just remember, take your time, and don't do anything reckless. Give them the opportunity to mess up, then capitalize. You have the speed, just keep a cool head out there."

"Got it!"

Just as they had finished speaking, the safety vehicle made its way off the track as the racers organized themselves in parallel lines.

"We'd like to give a special welcome to the number one car with driver Caleb Rafferty. A first timer on the circuit, joined by his family. He's been racing competitively since he was old enough to get behind the wheel. But this will be his first major event. We'll be keeping an eye on him, and we hope you do as well." The announcer proclaimed. Caleb felt a touch of embarrassment being put in the spotlight but felt a similar rush of excitement knowing his name was now on the tongues of thousands. *Is this what having real fame is like?* He wondered to himself. But before he could continue his fantasy, he and the other cars reached their predetermined speed of seventy-five miles per hour as they approached the acceleration point. Just then the radio crackled with static as a voice came through.

"You are green. Proceed to race speed."

In a clap of thunder, one by one, each of the racers jolted forward like a stampede of horses. Caleb found himself positioned at the fifteenth place but quickly moving forward as he deftly maneuvered through the other racers, like a hot knife through butter.

"You're killing it Caleb! You're closing up on eleventh place, just keep doing what you're doing." Sam exclaimed through the radio, failing to conceal his enthusiasm. Caleb was too focused to reply, but his mentor's words clung to him as he rounded the corner finishing up the second lap. Little was said as the race progressed.

Caleb kept his composure as he breezed past one opponent after another. By the fourth lap he had moved ahead a shocking nine positions landing him in sixth place.

"Amazing! New kid on the block, Caleb Rafferty is wasting no time moving ahead. With only fourteen laps remaining, if he keeps up this pace, he might just take home the gold!" The announcer exclaimed over an uproarious crowd. Three more laps came and went and suddenly Caleb found himself in third place following a sudden spin out from the number four car placed in front of him.

Caleb could not help but find it suspicious because it seemed to occur for no reason, as if some outside force had caused it. He spent no more than a fleeting moment pondering before pulling forward to close the distance between himself and the second position driver.

"Careful Caleb, start playing a little safe. The car coming up on you has a temper. He might try to swipe you to get ahead. Keep him blocked off until you can get ahead."

"Alright..." Caleb trailed off as he positioned himself to block the car that was quickly approaching. Then without warning, over the deafening roar of engines, a massive explosion rang out further down the track. Caleb quickly whipped his attention to the rear-view mirror as he saw an enormous billowing cloud of smoke.

"Ladies and gentlemen there have been a major accident! Seventeen drivers have been simultaneously disabled, we will be postponing the race until," the announcer proclaims solemnly before cutting off, "What the hell is that?"

As Caleb looked back into the mirror, he saw a shape burst forth from the massive fire on the track. Caleb was unable to make out exactly what it was, but it moved forward with impossible speed leaving behind bright sparks as it blazed down the asphalt. It closed up on the seventh position driver, then suddenly the car exploded into flames and spun out into the fence between the track and the hundreds of spectators. As it closed up, Caleb was suddenly able to fully see it. It was a car, but not just any car. It was the skeletal, burnt remains of the very car that Sebastian Alonzo drove on the fateful day he died. Its paint was scratched away leaving only a few splotches of its former glory, save for the number 06 which pulsed with an otherworldly glow on its sides. The metal frame was all rusted and bent up. From under its hood, smoke and fire bellowed out in hellish cascades of devilish light. Crackling sparks danced through the air as its naked rims grinded against the ground.

The impossibility of what he was witnessing sent Caleb into a panic before the muffled voice of Sam broke through the radio.

"Cale...you ha...out...there" The voice was broken up horribly with static as Caleb desperately tried to tune the radio frequency. "Off the track! You hear me!? Off the..." Once again, he was met only with static as the spine-chilling grinding sound of the phantasmal car crawling its way to him became louder and louder.

The demon wasted no time in climbing the ranks. As it sped past each and every driver in its path their vehicles were engulfed in a blaze and forced to careen into one another or the wall. Caleb's eyes were fully glued to the carnage behind him. He watched in horror as drivers desperately tried to escape their cars. Some were fortunate enough to escape, but he saw many cars rocking as the drivers scrambled to escape before the motions stopped without a sign of the driver. Caleb feared the worst and tried to keep himself focused on the road ahead of him to outrun the pursuer.

He took one last look behind him as the car encroached on the driver directly behind him. The driver behind him, Ryan Hanson, attempts to block out the ghost car by moving in front of it. However, his bold decision was not enough to deter the assailant. The car simply continued its war path as it accelerated into his rear bumper. In a final gambit, Ryan Hanson moves aside feigning to let it take his position, and as it moved forward, he retaliated and swiped to his side in attempt to disrupt it. Whether his decision was brave or foolish, it would prove to be his final. Caleb watched in horror as Ryan's tires collided with the ghost car's, the emanating heat coming forth from the demon began to melt the frame of his car into the driver's side, no doubt singing Hanson's flesh even through the flame-retardant suit.

Caleb couldn't hear his screams, but he knew he must have been in immense agony. Then with an impossible movement, the demon car twisted to the side with Hanson's car fused to it, and with a rapid jerk whipped it forward tearing it in half in a fiery explosion sending Ryan's bloodied burning corpse splattering along the asphalt. The rain of debris shot forward as if fired by a shotgun. Shards of burning metal cut through the fence into the crowd as scores of captivated spectators ran helplessly before being cut down.

The second position driver attempted to make his escape by steering away into the grass, but as he did a massive piece of debris from Hanson's car flew over Caleb and crashed down directly on top of him, sending him spinning into a fiery explosion. With his untimely demise, the only racers left were James Harlow in first, Caleb in second, and the phantasmal fury of Sebastian Alonzo in third. In an attempt to outrun the car, Caleb slams the accelerator and pushes his car forward through the smoke and debris and closes up on first place with the ghost chasing him closely.

Several tense seconds pass as the racers grind their tires against the asphalt. Then, seemingly frustrated, the ghost car makes another attack. The hood of the vehicle bursts upwards revealing the wreckage of an engine compartment roiling with smoke and fire. From the inferno, two twisted metals spears shoot forward. The first of which, barely misses Caleb's car taking out his side mirror and leaving a large gash down its side. James Harlow would not be so lucky. After reeling from his near-death experience, Caleb looked up just in time to see a massive metal spear pierced through the back of Harlow's car going straight through where his head would have been located.

Caleb watched helplessly as the car swerved back and forth before flipping on its side directly into the pit and crashing into the parked safety vehicle, leaving behind a burning wreckage and the screams of desperate workers scrambling to escape before they too were consumed by the spreading flames.

Overwhelming fear gripped Caleb as it occurred to him that his dream had become his nightmare. He was in first. But now, he had to survive against his last opponent. This was no longer a race for greatness, it was a race for his own life. He knew that anything short of first would mean certain death. So, with a burst of courage and desperation, he shifted into the next gear and pressed onward pulling slightly farther ahead than 06. Just as he started to regain hope, it was quickly dashed. As he sped forward, so did 06, Seemingly mimicking his own car's movements.

Caleb could hear the revving of its burnt-out engine as it jolted forward, colliding directly into his car's rear end, momentarily throwing it off balance. But thankfully to his fast reaction, Caleb managed to maintain control. It dawned on Caleb that it was going to be impossible to outrun this demon, so he held on tight and fought back against it as it continued to push into him, knocking his car off balance.

Unable to resist its onslaught, the beast pushed Caleb's car to the side and headlong into the concrete barrier with a solid crunch causing Caleb's head to bounce forward off the steering wheel. A wave of relief washed over him as his senses came back. The car had outmaneuvered him and now it would go on past him. Surely, he had made it out with his life. He lifted his head up and through his cracked visor he saw the devil charging at him once again. It had somehow reoriented itself, so it was once again facing him.

And it was charging forth with blinding speed. Caleb barely had enough time to clench up before he felt its immense impact against his side of the vehicle. It was surreal, like walking in a dream. His car was launched into the air, Parts from it detached themselves and rained upon the track. Caleb could only stare out helplessly as the sky spun around him swirling its colors with the asphalt before his car crashed down onto the asphalt with fury before proceeding to roll four times, scraping upside down across the finish line before finally coming to an abrupt stop on the grass near the maintenance bays.

When it came to a stop. Caleb was barely conscious but could smell the Bitter- Smell of the fuel which was leaking out of the gas tank and onto the ground. He unfastened his harness and fell onto the roof of the upturned car. His movement's slow and painful and knowing it wouldn't be long until the car went up in flames, he weakly booted the Damaged driver side door, at first it didn't budge a single bit, however, after a few more attempts, with the final mustering and using up the remaining strength he had, he booted it clean off of its hinges and crawled his way out onto the asphalt in which the car rested upon.

He could hear the roar of the ghost car's engine as he rolled over onto his back and looked over to the track, seeing it pass him by one final time before it vanished through a fiery – portal like gateway which appeared in the inner surface of the barriers which lined the stadiums safety fence. He slowly raised his hand and gripped his helmet tightly, ripping it off, letting it roll away from him as he stared up at the sky, which was bludgeoned by thick smoke and fire embers.

Caleb felt his consciousness slipping away from him as the immense pain took over all his senses. His vision pulsed black and red before fading to complete darkness. As he lay motionless, an emergency response team rapidly approached him and started to work on him right away, they thought they would surely loose him, but he responded briefly before passing out completely. All he could hear was the near inaudible chatter of the medical crew as well as the fire service who were by his side as well as the distant echo of sirens which blared in the distance, getting ever so closely. But that was it. That was all he could remember.

All that was left in the Ghost car's wake was death and destruction which would surely be pegged as one of the world's most devastating Race events.

Several weeks had passed since the events of the Sebastian Alonzo Memorial Race, now commonly referred to as the Hell Race by those who had witnessed it. Footage of the race was now infamous on the internet, seen by millions upon millions of morbidly curious watchers from all over the globes. Caleb had been out of the hospital for a few days at this point but has since spent his time in his office watching over the footage over and over again from every angle. Amy knocked on the door frame as she entered the room.

"Still can't sleep?"

"No..." He replied somberly.

"Well, you want anything for breakfast?"

"Not hungry..."

Amy's face dropped as she saw that she was not going to get anything substantial from him. "How're you feeling, today?"

"Like shit, same as every day since..."

"Babe..."

"Look, do you need something?" He said abruptly as he locked his bloodshot eyes on hers.

Amy said nothing. She just quickly exited the room struggling to cover up her tears. Caleb let out an exasperated sigh as he slowly pushed his wheelchair up to the door and slowly closed it behind her, leaving his alone in his darkened room with the only light coming from his computer. He looked around the room and took notice of how empty it looked now that he'd had Amy throw out all of his old memorabilia except for newspaper clippings crudely hung up in their place. In a way, racing was still his obsession. But now that he'd been declared permanently paralyzed from the waist down, he shifted his focus from the actual act of racing to trying to come to terms with what happened that fateful day.

As he watched the clip of his car being mauled by the phantom, he felt lightheaded and nauseous. He may have survived the encounter, but he felt his life was thoroughly over now that his dreams had been crushed along with the car. For him, at least there was some cruel irony in that he did what he set out to do. He won the race and certainly made a name for himself as the sole survivor of the most gruesome racing accident in the history of the sport.

THE END

CASE NINE

SUBMECHANOPHOBIA

A BRILLIANT GOLDEN sunset peered over the cliffside reflecting off the gentle ebb and flow of waves below. An old Volkswagen van chugged along upwards around the bend as its three passengers look out onto the scenic vista. A well-built man with a stubbly beard and military-buzzcut drives the van. Thomas Stevenson tried to keep his eyes on the road but found his eyes drifting, distracted by the view. Alex Whiteford sits in the seat directly behind him facing out through the passenger window. He is tall with an average build and has medium length brown hair parted to his right side.

He looks over to his girlfriend Denver as she continues to talk over the phone. Denver was only a bit shorter than Alex with an average frame. Her ginger hair tied up in a bun and her blue eyes focused out towards the water that glistened hundreds of feet below. She adjusts her nose piercing with her free hand and continues to speak confidently to her 'Man on the inside' over the phone.

"So, you're sure this place is legit, right?" She asked with a hint of disease in her tone. Alex looked over to catch her gaze as she looked back at him. He gave her a faint smile as he leaned his head over to look long into the abyss below them over the cliffside. She simply nodded her head rhythmically, as if satisfied by what she was hearing from the other end. "Great, thanks... Yeah, I'll give you a call when we're leaving."

"So, what's the deal?" Thomas piped up from the driver's seat. Denver looked at him as she placed the phone in her jacket pocket and answered.

"Well, our man on the inside just finished making sure the coast was clear. So, he'll let the security guards know he's clocked in and on watch, then he'll let us through. We'll go in, do our thing, leave and no one will be any the wiser." She replied confidently.

"This will be the best three hundred dollars we ever spent Can you imagine what we'll see down there. No one's been down there in over a decade; it's bound to have some cool stuff worth something." Alex chimed in.

After approximately a half hour more of driving they pull up to the front gate and see the rusty, faded sign past all the caution tape and wire fencing which read, "THE DEPTHS OCEANIC THEME PARK". It was originally designed as an educationally focused interactive exhibit where people could experience a deep dive and come into contact with animatronic marine life which was supposed to talk to the divers and tell them about their ecosystem and what have you. However, nearly ten years ago it closed suddenly and decisively for officially unknown reasons.

Rumors spread like wildfire at first saying that one of the machines went haywire and seriously injured someone, but of course ancient rumors alone were not enough to deter three intrepid, rogue divers. Thomas brought the van to a slow stop as they approached the front gate where a figure stood waiting for them, strongly silhouetted by the van's headlights. As they approached and came to a halt, they realized it was a man in a security guard's uniform. Denver's 'inside man.' As he noticed the van, he made his way over to them.

"So, you're the guests? Park just closed; you know." He said with a touch of sarcasm.

"Well, I'm sure the fish won't mind if we poke around after hours." Thomas said extending his hand out of the window handing over a small envelope containing three-hundred dollars for their entry.

"Yeah, well, just be sure you're out in two hours, okay? Second shift shows up around then, and if we get caught, we're all fucked, got it?" He said bluntly as he counted the money in the envelope.

"You won't even know we were here." Alex said jokingly as he stepped out of the van.

As the guard began walking away the trio went to the back of the van to gather their gear and made their way through the gate which the guard had left slightly ajar for them to go through. As Thomas went to the front of the van to shut it off, Alex couldn't help but notice that its headlights had illuminated a large, reflective yellow sign which read

"WARNING: This facility is unstable. Trespassers have the potential to experience bodily injury and/or death. Entry is forbidden and is monitored by local authorities."

Alex felt a slight sense of anxiety start welling up in him as the van headlights cut out, leaving the large building illuminated only by the humming, fluorescent lights of the guard posts. As the trio entered through the front gate, they were taken aback by its scale. It was totally massive, almost like a small city. Their flashlights cut across signs for smaller attractions and concession stands. Years of wear and tear had done quite a bit of damage to the whole park. Everything was falling apart and coated in rust. It was a bit eerie, they felt, to be there in the dead of night with only each other as company and the lingering spirits of a once exciting and lively world.

Of course, they had little time to admire the tragic beauty of the ghostly shell. They were there for one thing, and one thing alone: The Abyss; one hundred meters of dark water lined with defunct animatronics and winding underwater hallways. They knew there would be little of value that they could take as souvenirs, but the memory and experience of the forbidden dive would be more than enough for the three of them.

Eventually they stumble upon a dusty sign which reveals the path to their destination. With their efforts now coming to fruition, the trio picked up their pace, each of them hoping to be the first to lay eyes on it. Along the way, they took small detours into the rotting shops picking up stray t-shirts and stuffed dolls of the park's mascot, a cute, cartoonish shark affectionately named Titan.

"Hey, what do you really think is going to be in there? Do you think there's just going to be floating robots in the water, or do you think they took everything with them when they packed-up and shut the place down?" Denver questioned aloud.

"Honestly, there's probably nothing worthwhile. But we won't know until we go down and have a look, will we?" Thomas replied sharply.

"What if all the fish down there were still working? Just telling each other fun fish facts for years on end." Alex jokingly added.

After a few more minutes of trekking through the building, they approached the end of their pilgrimage. The largest building on the park's campus by a significant portion, with its roof cracked and broken, paint chipped and faded, and a massive sign featuring the cartoon shark which read The Abyss. This was it; this was main attraction. Luckily for the group, its main doors had rusted and broken off their hinges, leaving the portcullis unobstructed with its siren song louder than ever.

They looked upon it with mouths agape, admiring its three-story height and perfectly circular dome structure.

"You all know the rumors about this place, right?" Alex asked quietly.

"About how a couple people got hurt and that they closed the park because of it?" Thomas replied.

", according to our contact, they're not just rumors. He claims that he worked here when it happened. Apparently, the main animatronic went berserk when it was supposed to "feed" on the other animatronic as part of the ride. He said it just floated over to a group and started attacking, and I guess not all of them survived." Denver said somberly.

"Did they just scrap the thing?" Alex asked.

"I have no idea. For obvious reasons, the park owners did all they could to keep the whole ordeal covered up. There were also some very outlandish theories, one of which is that a former employee, who was a dark magic practitioner, was pissed about being fired and placed a curse on the shark and that's what made it go crazy."

"So, there's a chance a possessed shark animatronic could still be down there?" Thomas replied cynically, "Come on, that's absurd. If that was true, which is laughable, why wouldn't they just try to sell all their assets, demon sharks included. Would be worth a good bit of cash"

"I mean, if you're scared Thomas, feel free to just keep watch outside." Alex said as he patted him on the back condescendingly.

"Oh, I'm definitely shitting myself...Shut up, Alex." Thomas replied as the three of them shared a brief laugh. As they ventured onwards into The Abyss, they came across a wall lined with dusty framed photos taken of people in the water with the animatronic shark. The three were silently shocked when they saw what it looked like.

The plushies and shirts they stashed in their backpacks did little justice for the real thing. It was a whopping sixteen feet in length and twice their length in diameter. As opposed to the cutesy cartoonish smile on the mascot, the actual Titan's face was cold and mechanical. Its eyes were lifeless and a deep, glassy black. The resemblance to a real shark was uncanny but there was no beauty in it as one might perceive in a living shark of its size. Instead, it was deeply unsettling to see with all of its moving joints and sheet metal skin.

The three exchanged unnerved glances as they wondered what it might look like now if it experienced the same about of rot and decay as the rest of the park.

They tried not to be too shaken, and made their way down to the main atrium of the facility and took the time to change into their diving gear as they stood at a closed door which bore a large sign which read

"CLOSED DUE TO FLOODING".

"This must be it, the shark maze. If there's anything worth salvaging, it'll be in here." Denver said as she showed the door open with an ear-piercing screech as it raked against the floor.

The trio walked the length of the large circular room and shone their lights all around revealing mostly torn up posters and decaying paint.

They stood at the precipice of the massive pool which served as the entry way to the maze that housed Titan and the other animatronics. The water was absolutely still, and only barely evaporated, which seemed strange to the group but not enough for anyone to make note of it to the others. The only thing of note in the murky water was a capsized passenger submarine, which looks as though it could fit eleven to thirteen passengers in it. It must have been one of the ride's underwater carriers which was likely used to transport guests through the underwater abyss.

One by one, the three took to the water. It was difficult to see anything in the water despite all of them having bright lights attached to their suits and headpieces which also included earpieces and small microphones so that they would be able to speak to one other. They swam together close, speaking about how crazy what they were doing was as they pushed aside small pieces of debris and small, fake fish which seemed to float in place. Admiring the technical marvel of the underwater railings and infrastructure. Eventually, they came across a large central area that split off into four tunnels. With the railings which must have carried the submarine vessel following a one-way like system through the tunnels. Satisfied that a killer, cursed shark was nowhere to be seen they decide that it would be safe to split up to cover more ground.

Denver went down the left most tunnel which followed a series of winding hallways and avenues. Eventually she found herself in a dead-end room and as she scoured the corners, she decided there was nothing more to see and turned to head back to go down a different pathway. However, as she does, she spins herself around and feels her head bump against something hard the impact giving her a fright.

She looks up and examines a massive figure that had been obscured by the darkness. It was Titan. She was sure of it, and as she swam along its length, she examined its black, lifeless eyes and noted that its side had been torn open revealing its mechanical skeleton and motor systems. Excitedly, she spoke to the others via Her earpiece to alert them of her discovery.

"Alex, Thomas. Can you hear me?" she asked as her Excitement struggled to contain itself. There was a second of silence before a hiss sounded in her ears.

"Yeah, I'm here." said Alex.

"You bet, why wouldn't I be?" said Thomas with a laugh.

"You are not going to believe what I've just found."

"What have you found? An old pin worth a couple of grand?" Thomas answered sarcastically.

"Shut it, in what appears to be a maintenance bay of some sort, I found Titan. Y'know, the killer demon shark that has, by the looks of it, been left here and forgotten."

"Your fucking kidding?" responded Alex with utter surprise, Thomas remained silent.

"I'm not, it's really here and could be worth a fortune!" -she said knowing she needed their help to figure out what to do with it. With her back turned to the mechanical beast, she was completely oblivious to the fact that its eyes began flickering with a dull red glow, it's mouth stretching wide open, displaying it's rows upon rows of razor sharp teeth before fading back to black, resetting it's posture.

After receiving the update from Denver, Thomas and Alex began making their way to her, following her instructions and guidance carefully, but out of nowhere and so suddenly, The Abyss awakened with the sudden flash of lights all around them from the fixtures placed in the maze, they hear several sharp pings ringing out from the surface as red lights spun around them like a warning signs. Then, just as quickly as they came on, The Abyss fell back into its deep slumber.

"Did you guys see that?" Denver asked nervously.

"Yeah, are you guys close to the entrance of the maze? I think we need to get out of here." Thomas replied.

"Denver, I see you, look over here." Alex said as he waved to the black figure that moved slowly before dashing away in the opposite direction.

"What are you talking about, I just met up with Thomas. Where are you?"
Alex looked around intensely back to where he saw the shadow in the water but saw nothing.

"Sorry, thought I seen something just ahead of me, probably just saw my own shadow. I'm on my way back to where you guys are. "after several tense minutes, the trio are reunited uneventfully as they begin to come up with a plan. Alex not even questioning as to how he and Thomas got split up to begin with.

"I think we should get out of here; this place is seriously starting to give me the creeps. I mean what could have triggered that alarm? And what could have caused the place to light up like that?" Alex said.

"I don't fucking know, but it shouldn't have happened." Said Thomas with an uneasy tone. Denver looked at the pair and gave her thoughts.

"I swear to fuck, see if that fucker has sold us out. I'll kill him myself. I think we need to get out of here."

"What after traveling all those miles? And paying a large sum of cash? Nah, we aren't leaving until we have something worth value. It's what we do, now buckle up, we're staying!"

"Thomas, Get a grip. The alarms and security system aren't going to just trigger on their own, someone obviously has set it off. That will ping a response to the closest police station and they will be out pretty quickly to see what's going on" She responded impatiently.

Thomas looked at her surprised by her nippy response. Something that was out of character for her, but it was a small wake up call to him that they may be heading for trouble.

"Let's just take it easy. We should make our way back to where we dived and just go, we can always come back at a later date. It's not worth the consequences we could be facing for entering." Alex concluded as the others simply nodded their head in confirmation.

they made their way to the surface and as they breached, they saw that the entry way they came in through was inexplicably sealed off. The doors which had been off their hinges now appeared fixed perfectly back in place. Thomas made his way over to the doors first but found them thoroughly locked shut.

"Well, fuck. What do we do now? Should we call that guard guy for help?" Thomas said exasperated.

"I don't think he'll answer, and besides, I've got no signal down here." Denver said as she checked her phone from her backpack which had been left on the patio net to the pool entry point.

"I saw a sign that pointed out an emergency exit while we were down there. Why don't we just stick together and go that way?" Alex chimed in with renewed enthusiasm.

The others nodded in agreement, and with that they descended back into the darkness of the water. The three swam in close proximity so as not to lose sight of one another as they followed the arrows pointing to an emergency exit. They each looked around with great apprehension, though from what exactly, they were unsure. However, their vague dread quickly gave way to abject horror as a massive shadow began to peer out from around a corner from an adjoining tunnel just in front of them.

They stared in silent horror as the figures glowing red eyes moved from side to side searching the area and heard it let out a mechanical noise from its open maw, Denver knew straight away what it was, but couldn't make sense as to how it was even possible. Titan was now in motion. She struggled to speak as she watched the two red glowing orbs got closer; it was feeding time for Titan.

Shocked and unable to move, the three floated in place, as still as they possibly could, and in the process, turned off the mask mounted flashlights plunging them into darkness as the large mechanical frame glided slowly over their heads by mere inches. The intimidating noise of its inner workings slightly bludgeoned out by the water and gear they wore. Just as fast as it had appeared, it was gone, disappearing into the darkness of the abyss's tunnels.

"Holy Fuck," Spouted Thomas. "How the fuck is that even possible? Is it even possible?"

"We need to be careful. Take our time and stay together. As one slip up could bring it back to us. It was clearly attracted to our flashlights. And must have been following us for a while." Said Denver as her voice lowered its tone to a near whisper. She gripped Alex's arm tightly as he turned to face the two.

"We should just move slowly as you said, stick to the side walls and we should be able to avoid it, as its eyes are a dead giveaway to where it is."

"Agreed." Said both Thomas and Denver in sync with one another. That was it. The trio remained together as they navigated a few of the under-water tunnels, including a few maintenance tunnels. But it wasn't to last. As they reach a large

before watching as Titan caught sight of them and then began to swim furiously towards them. With this, the three began to swim away as quickly as they possibly could down the tunnel they had been following. Hearing each other's panicked breathing and muttering, Denver suddenly unleashed a blood-curdling scream. Alex stopped in place and looked back to see that she had been caught by the beast. It had her leg caught in its mechanical jaw and he saw as it began to robotically thrash her around with her blood mixing violently in the murky water.

He and Thomas swam back as fast as they could and with Thomas pushing on its face and Alex pulling Denver, they were able to free her. Titan was still thrashing, as if unaware that its meal had been removed, and using this opportunity, they swam away with

Denver holding tight onto Alex. They come across a small entry way just wide enough for them to get through one at a time and decide that it's their best bet for now since Titan would be unable to fit through the tunnel. Alex helps Denver get through first, then he and Thomas hear the pained robotic shriek of Titan as they turn to see it barreling towards them with its eyes burning a glowing red. Thomas quickly begins pushing Alex into the tunnel and says,

"Go! Keep an eye on Denver, I'm going to try to lead it away!" as he begins paddling violently away.

Alex pauses from within the tunnel and can only watch as the mechanical beast blows past him towards its prey. It isn't long before they hear his agonizing screams along with the sound of blood being coughed up before his radio goes completely silent. Fighting back waves of nausea, Alex has no choice but to turn away from the bloodbath and paddles his way back to a wounded Denver.

He takes hold of her hand and begins to swim through the thin tunnel before it lets out into a large open area. A flicker of hope appears in them as they realize they might have stumbled upon another exit and begin to make their way to the surface. However, their hope quickly gives way to dread as Titan emerges at Mach speed from a separate tunnel. Alex sees that its jaws are now painted in Thomas's blood as it spills away from the hole in its side and feels a mixture of grief and horror as he realizes what happened to Thomas is about to happen to them.

The two are unable to breach the surface before they are set upon by Titan and it once again grabs hold of the already bloodied Denver and begins to gnash its mechanical jaws around the legs. Her panicked cries of agony send Alex's mind into retreat as he frantically looks around for anything to help. His only hope is large floating piece of debris that he grabs hold of and makes a charge towards the behemoth. In a desperate lunge, he plunged the pointed end into Titan's glowing eye. His gambit a success, it momentarily stops Titan, sparks emit from the socket as it begins jerking in place violently, before shutting down and lifelessly floating in the blood tainted – murky water.

This give him just enough time to grab hold of Denver, who was losing consousness quickly and make a break for the surface. There is only enough time for him to help Denver out of the water as just mere feet below them, the shark's eyes begin to flicker intimately before it opens and slams it's jaws shut, coming to life once more, and it's not long after he feels the impossible grip of Titan take hold of his oxygen tank and yank him back down into the abyss. As it dragged him further and further down, he begins to choke with his oxygen supply now eviscerated. As his muscles begin convulsing, his shaking hands are able to let loose the tank from his back as he hurriedly made his ascent. His mind raced, he knew if caught again there would be no more saving grace.

He would suffer the same grisly fate as his friend and with a final shove he burst through the surface of the water and paddled to the edge to pull himself up with the help of Denver, who used what small energy she had left to help him up. As he crawled to safety, he and Denver saw as Titan's jagged dorsal fin pierced through the water one last time before descending back into its nightmarish slumber.

Finally, free from their pursuer, both collapse to their knees, with Denver's condition stable, but far from good, the pair embrace one another and mourn their friend through heavy frightened tears. They resolve to go and turn themselves in so that they can get medical attention. They knew they might face dire consequences for their trespassing of a dangerous condemned property, and even more so, for unexplainable disappearance of Thomas Stevenson. They worried greatly about how they would tell their story, knowing full well the truth would be impossible for anyone to comprehend. But deep down, they were thankful to walk away from The Abyss with their lives.

They wondered though, what could have brought that beast to life. Was it a simple malfunction within its programming that had somehow reactivated? Or was there some truth to the rumor that foul magics had breathed life into its mechanical skeleton. For Denver and Alex, the truth might never reveal itself, and for them that felt like the best option.

THE END

CASE TEN

Alone

The gentle patter of rain outside Alice Wishart's Bungalow turned into a cacophonous barrage of heavy water droplets on glass accompanied by the booming cracks of thunder and lightning. The Scottish Highlands that surround her are as treacherous during a storm as they are gorgeous in the glistening morning sunlight that follows. A sudden flash of lightning illuminates the dimly lit household and sends a jolt down Alice's spine. Deaf from birth, she is unable to hear the thunder, but is still startled by the lightning. She glances reflexively out of her living room window to see the trees whipping violently in the rain, and quickly turns away back to the gentle warmth of her fireplace. She extends a hand to her side but stops suddenly.

She knew the hand she was reaching for wasn't there anymore. She looks over to the opposite side of the loveseat and finds it painfully empty. A steady stream of tears rolls down her face as she turns away and picks up a small, framed photograph from the coffee table next to her.

The face that looked back at her was the smiling, handsome face of Darren Wishart, her late husband. The second world war had come to its conclusion only three months ago, but he had been claimed by its bloodied flames almost a full year ago. The photo was from their wedding day. She studied his face and his outfit, running her fingers down the glass frame as if to touch him. She compared the glowing woman in the photo to the dulled woman in the small mirror that hung on the opposite wall. She thought about how long it must have been since she felt as happy as she looked in that photo. She also wondered if she'd ever feel that way again.

"I miss you so much, Darren... I wish you were here. You'd hold me and tell me to not look so miserable with that cocky smile on your face... I'm struggling... I really am." She thought to herself as she stared at the photo. She let out a gloomy sigh and carefully placed it back down.

Another flicker of lightning against the blackened sky once again caused her to jump. She imagined that maybe that was Darren trying to tell her "Pick yourself up, woman!" She let out a sharp exhalation and realized it was time to get back to work now that the mood was right.

She lifted herself up from her seat and looked down the hallway only barely lit by the faint glow of dull electric lights that lined the walls. She had been afraid of the dark ever since she was a little girl and it was a trait that Darren had always teased her about. Even still, he would sign that everything was okay and that he wouldn't let anything hurt her as they'd go down the shadowy hallways of their home, hand in hand. It made her feel safe back then, but now without him she had to put the lights out and traverse the darkness alone.

She flicked the switch and the lights went out. She began to move with a decent pace keeping her eyes fixated on her bedroom door so as not to linger in the shadows. However, as she passed by the door to her husband's workspace, she noticed that the door was wide open. She found this curious since she never opened that door anymore. She stopped herself to peer into the room but saw nothing out of the ordinary. Seeing his tools patiently waiting where he left made her feel uneasy. In a way, Alice felt a connection to those tools and trinkets. She, too, was waiting for him to come back so that they might continue to work on the life they had started to build.

She hung her head briefly then went to close the door. She indulged herself one final look and noticed a dark silhouette in the corner of the room just before the catch clicked shut. She held the door's handle for a second, thinking about what she saw, but rationalized that it must have merely been her own shadow from the candle's light behind her. She resolved to hurry back to her bedroom fearing that her mind would continue to torment her with false apparitions.

Alice breathed a sigh of relief as she closed the bedroom door behind her and turned on the light. She felt a small relief being there, it was the one place she could lie her head down to dream of her beloved and escape the cruel reality of her life. It was also where she turned her thoughts into art. Alice worked as a writer and made decent money through a local publisher. Despite being easily frightened, her passion was in the macabre and as such she wrote gothic and horror fiction which was well received by the publisher's readers. She held a natural talent to paint pictures through words and drew inspiration from the things in life that scared her, and in doing so found catharsis. Alice traipsed slowly to her typewriter and glanced over her sketches and notes for her newest and most personal novel to date. She read over the title of her work carefully, The Woman in White by Alice Wishart. At its core, it was a story about a woman struck by tragedy who experience a haunting. She was used to writing more esoteric pieces, whereas this was far more heavy-handed. But this story was not just another ghost story; this was autobiographical, and to her, this was her singular way to cope with the death of the one man she ever truly loved.

Minutes turn to hours as Alice notices that it was well past midnight by the time her eyelids became heavy and decided she had made enough progress on the story to call it a night. She placed her face in her hands and rubbed her face. She was completely exhausted since her nights for the past several weeks had been largely sleepless save for a few hours here and there. She feared tonight might be the same, and that another sleepless night would vex her.

As her head becomes heavy in her hands and she feels as though she might be in the embrace of sleep, a shadow begins to move along the wall. A spectral, pale hand peels away from the dark silhouette and reaches for her as it gently grips her shoulder, then vanishes. Suddenly she is shaken back into alertness and quickly looks around her room, startled by the invisible force. She rubs her eyes and slowly rises from her seat. She only had her eyes closed for a few minutes but felt as though she had been asleep for hours feeling the groggy sensation as she meandered to her window.

She pulled the blinds aside and watched as the storm outside continued to rage on. Suddenly, the notices the lights behind her all flicker and vanish. She whipped around quickly and was suddenly confronted with utter blackness save for the dull light of the fireplace that was beginning to fade away. After a moment, her blood ran cold as she realized she had closed her bedroom door but was now able to see through the opened frame into the shroud of darkness down her hallway. She felt herself begin to shake as she sidled clumsily over to the small hand lantern on top of the wardrobe, keeping her eyes fixed on the darkened hallway.

After some struggle getting it because of her height compared to the wardrobes she was able to grab it and light it. Then she looked feverishly around the dancing shadows of the room as the lantern's light shook in her quivering hands. With a rush of bravery and morbid curiosity she began making her way out of the bedroom towards the living room.

As she cautiously moved through the hallway, she continued looking around at every moving shadow unsure whether it was just a trick of the light or something sinister. She makes her way into the living room which is only dimly illuminated by the smoldering ash of the fireplace. She tries the light switch to no avail and then notices something out of place from the corner of her eye.

She sees a window is wide open with the curtains swaying wildly in the wind. She anxiously moves over to it in order to close it but finds herself looking outwards into the tree line near her house. Amidst the downpour she sees a strange shape. A bolt of lightning cracks out and lights up the sky and reveals the strange figure by the trees for a brief moment.

Alice is instantly stricken with panic and dread as she makes out the being before her. It is a woman with skin as white as paper, wearing a long white gown billowing softly against the stormy wind, her hair is jet black and vaguely covers her face, but even still, Alice can see that her eyes are empty save for an inky blackness. The being that was standing before her was The Woman in White from her book. But just as the light vanished from the sky, so too did the apparition. Alice stood there in shock for a moment before slowly backing away with her mouth agape.

The visage of the woman now burned into her mind, the woman was created in Alice's likeness so that she could assert herself into her story, but seeing its ghastly appearance sent her mind into retreat as she struggled to make sense and decide what to do next. She turned her head into the kitchen and saw the phantasm standing there in the darkness. Alice yelped in horror as she dropped the lantern to the floor, extinguishing the last light she had.

Just as the light vanished, the ghost disappeared once again. Alice was now without sight or sound as she picked herself up, and with her hands shaking violently she began feeling around in the darkness. A feeling washed over Alice that she needed to find shelter away from her pursuer and she quietly made her way to the hallway.

She found herself in front of a small room that was being built to become a nursery for when she and Darren became pregnant. She pulled herself inside after seeing that it was empty. She looked around the unfinished room and took notice of the crib that Darren had built. Despite being wrought with fear, she now felt a deep depression. They had been trying for a child before he went away to war; she vividly recalled one of their last conversations had been about what they'd name their child if it were a boy or a girl.

Suddenly she notices the crank on the music box sitting on a shelf begin to move on its own. She wonders for a moment what its song must sound like then begins to walk over to investigate. Just as she sticks her hand out to silence it, it suddenly falls violently to the ground and shatters. Startled she quickly backs away out of the room and feels a chilling breeze brush over her. She looks over to its source and through the darkness, she sees the woman staring at her from the entry way of her bedroom. Alice sees it open its mouth as if unhinged at the jaw and begin to float menacingly towards her. Alice can only gasp out in horror then decides to make a break for her husband's workspace hoping to escape through the window. But as she wraps her fingers around the knob she turns to no avail as it had somehow become stuck.

She continues to push and shove the door watching the apparition move ever closer to her. Alice feels her heartbeat pulsing in her ears as she feverishly assaults the door, then finally bursts through it, and slams it shut behind her. She watches the door for a moment, but sees nothing, wondering if the woman was still waiting for her outside. She turns to the window hoping to finally make her escape. However, just as she goes to open the window, she is confronted by the pale visage of the woman staring at her from directly outside.

Alice falls backwards and begins to hysterically panic. She thinks about her husband and what he would do to protect her now. She thinks about his funeral and how hard she cried then. Then she is assaulted with an image in her mind, like a memory that didn't belong to her; she witnesses as Darren is mowed down in a hail of gunfire. His blood spraying out like crimson rain as his lifeless body hits the muddy ground with his bloodshot eyes facing upwards.

Alice shakes her head trying to make the images go away then she is again assailed by cruel memories of her time in the hospital. A few months before Darren deployed, Alice became pregnant and the day he left he signed to her about how excited he would be to see his child when he came back. However, only several weeks after he left, she miscarried and spent several days alone in the hospital. She wanted to write him a letter but found out not much longer that he had perished.

Alice sat there curled in the fetal position, a sobbing mess, having confronted her most painful memories and fantasies of her husband's death. Slowly her tears began to fade away as she realized she had nothing left to lose in her life, except for her life. She yet lived and felt somehow that Darren would have told her that her life wasn't over, and that she needed to get up and face her demons. She carefully stood up and steadied her resolve. She walked calmly to the door, and slowly opened it.

The woman in white stood directly in the doorway and stared back at her through blackened eyes. Alice hesitated for a moment but pushed her fears aside and walked directly past her. To her surprise, the woman did not stop her. Instead, she merely moved aside and began floating wistfully behind her. Alice made her way into the nursery and picked up a small teddy bear that was meant for their child, then she began looking around the house. Every corner and every wall were lined with memorabilia that tied her down.

Every picture filled her with grief and dragged all of her sorrow to the surface. She realized in that moment if she were to ever be free of what truly haunted her, she needed to let go of what kept her tethered. She turned to the specter in the hallway and began to sign to it, "it's time to move on."

In that moment, the entity's eyes turned from an angry blackness to a somber pale blue, just like her own. As Alice looked on to the ghost, she realized that she was simply the manifestation of her guilt and sadness, and now with her mind made up she was ready to let go of her inner darkness and move on to a brilliant bright future.

The ghost wrapped its arms around her in a warm embrace then dissipated just as quickly as she had appeared.

Alice gathered whatever possessions she could carry in a bag and made one final trip to the fireplace where she started a roaring fire. Then with the tongs, she grabbed hold of one of the burning logs and with immeasurable strength she launched it into the wall and watched as its flames began to overtake the house. She made a hasty exit through the front door and turned to watch from the safety of the tree line. As the house was engulfed in the inferno it began to crumble and turn to ash despite the still pouring rain.

She noticed from her bedroom window the woman in white reappear and stare into her one last time. And with her spectral gaze, Alice fell into a deep slumber. During her sleep she experienced a dream that felt as real as anything possibly could.

In this dream, she was standing in the sun with the rubble of her home still smoldering from the blaze. Only now she was not alone. She looked to her side and saw Darren holding a small child by the hand as they began to walk up to her, Alice making her way over to them. Darren handed over the small child to her and began to sign to her.

"This is our daughter; she looks just like you. Her name is Emily and she's been waiting to see you for a while." He signed.

Alice looked down at the child and smiled brilliantly as the little girl looked back up glowing with joy. For the first time, she was able to know the love of her child. Though bittersweet, she felt at peace as she held her husband's hand with the child gently tucked in the other. The family turned towards the house and simply watched as the ashes rose up towards the sun-soaked sky. "I'll see you again someday, so go out and live until then. I love you." Darren signed to her, then Alice awoke to the gentle rain still dancing on her face as the daylight broke over the tree line with the fire that consumed the house now reduced to thin trails of smoke.

Months since then pass with Alice's story of the woman in white becoming a smashing success. But she takes one last trip to the remains of the house that had once been her home. However, now she is able to look upon it in quiet joy as she reminisces about the happiness that once lined its walls. She feels somewhat sad but is renewed now and feels ready to move on with her life, complacent to know that one day she will be reunited with those she loves.

She thinks to herself of the final lines in her book,

* * *

"And in that moment, I gazed into the fire as it washed away the grief, the loss, the pain, and the sadness that hung over me. The rubble that was left would be the starting point of a new life, a life of happiness, love, and joy. The woman in white wasn't malevolent entity, she was nothing more than an otherworldly guide, pulling me from the ever-expanding ocean of grief before I drowned. Life is pure, and now, I can move on. Watch over me my love, until we meet again."

* * *

A final tear is shed as she walks back to the black Car behind her and gets in. As the car pulls away from the remains, she takes a single glance back, seeing the woman in white stare her down before vanishing a final time. Alice allows a subtle smile to play at her lips as the car turns away from the house before taking off down the dirt path toward civilization.

The End

DEAR READER,

FIRSTLY, I'd like to take the small but huge (To me) opportunity to say thank you. Thank you for picking up this small step in a larger journey and for taking a chance on me, A newcomer in the word of creative writing. I also want to thank you, as a reader, for standing with these characters all the way to the end and experiencing their tales for yourself. The Paranormal Origins Universe is only getting started!

Thank You,

Liam

CREDITS

FIRST OFF, I'd like to take this opportunity to thank two important people for their work on this book. Firstly, My Editor and now good friend, **Robert Frank**. Thank you for standing by as I adjusted the stories and all the long hours and days you worked with me to help bring them to life, even more so that your way of editing is solid and how you were able to pick up on many things I missed. Here's to a long-lasting creative Duo-ship and congratulations on your marriage!

SECONDLY, I'd like to Give a Huge shout out to my Talented Artist on this book and many more to come; **Jusep Kurnia**. The art for the book was something I was worried about for a long time, and after being failed by multiple artists, I came across Jusep, I sent the sketches and documents away for how I wanted them to look, and the final illustrations (The ones present before each story) were more than I could ever have asked for and left me stunned.

THANK YOU, Guys, for helping me make this book a reality and for all the time and effort each of you put in to help me tell these stories. Now I'm going to mention those who have supported me both in my writing and in my life, all of whom gave me the support and padding to start my journey as a writer.

***

NOW THAT I HAVE THANKED the guys that helped me bring these characters and stories to life in this book, I'd now like to list and thank a good lot of people who have supported me both in my personal life and writing (as well as my other ventures)

***

FIRSTLY, I'D LIKE TO THANK my family; **My Mum and Dad**, who has been my rock whenever things have gone wrong and when I felt like I was at rock bottom and had nothing left. Thank you for all the support over the years, a debt I can't repay. Even though you've had your own battles, you always do your best for me and That's something I won't ever forget. Secondly, my dad who along with my mum was always there and supported everything I've done and always pushed me to pursue my own path.

MY SIBLINGS Claire (Polly & Darren) For being the run of the mill older sibling, and brother in Law, Who've been there for me and supported me throughout the years and who has stood by my work, even when I thought I'd fail. And pushed me when I refused to move, thanks for all the laughs and support Polly and Darren, my brother Mark, who I didn't really get to know too well, however, before his passing , what we had meant a lot to me and the kind words you gave me hit home.

I'D ALSO LIKE TO THANK Andrew for standing in and supporting my work and being there for me and for supporting my mum during times of hardship. Thank you!

NOW I'M GOING TO THANK all of the following For their support over the years; Kellie Anne O'Neil and her family who have supported all my ventures, myself and my family over the years (Even helping out with my debut film and taking on two of the roles)

NEXT UP IS Mags, Julie, David and their families, all of whom have kept in the loop and supported the book.

I'D ALSO LIKE TO THANK Jake Brown for his support over the past few months and for being an all - round good guy, who, alongside others(Jamie, Ben, DJ and Warren also) have been giving feedback on the book (Cover, Concepts and Ideas) over the course of it's creation and for being positive toward its final Release and standing by me during the tough times that occurred during this books creation.

ALSO, A SPECIAL MENTION to Jake O'Brien for his support over the books final few weeks, receiving feedback from you was a lot of help, I'd like to have you work with me in the future or on another project, Keep up the good work with your illustrations!

AND TO ALL THOSE who I have worked with in College and graduated With, the folk that I took the first steps with into the creative industries, Film and TV Class of 2016- 2019 (Connor, Laura, Carrie, James, Marc, Savannah, Shannon, Emelia, Maxine, George, Sean, Connor M, Hannah, Claire, Linda, Jordanne, and my lecturers; Alan, Michael, Kim, Alec and Tommy, Tom, Holly, David and Jordan) Thanks For working with me to help bring my ideas to life and for a fantastic few years!

ABOUT THE AUTHOR

Liam Kenny Downie (Born 22nd of january,1998) is a Scottish Filmmaker, screenwriter and indie author primarily focusing on Horror and Suspense. Liam was born and raised for the first half of his life in the town of Cumbernauld, with his current years residing the village of Salsburgh, North Lanarkshire. He was raised by his mother Margaret, and his father, James, as well as his four siblings, Claire (Polly) Darren, Steven and Mark. From a young age, he had always aspired to create worlds and tell stories which ultimately led to him writing his first short story "V Sabre" A Sci-fi tale inspired by the likes of Star Wars and Halo The story won him his first creative writing award which fueled his passion even more, ultimately leading him to write many more shorts which were lost to time, however, upon completing his six years at caldervale High school, he then took the next step in his creative journey. A film course at New College Lanarkshire.

It was during his time at NCL, he earned his craft in writing (Primarily screenplays) Filmmaking techniques and editing. As well as this, he also penned his first ever short film The Rain Man and would finally go on to write and direct multiple short films with Some gaining attention in the media. He now Primarily focuses on writing novels and collections in his "Paranormal Origins Anthology" Playing videogames or spending time with family.

Printed in Great Britain
by Amazon

74178439R00102